WHISKEY REBEL

WHISKEY REBEL

JEFFREY DUNN

IZZARD INK
PUBLISHING®

IZZARD INK PUBLISHING
PO Box 522251
Salt Lake City, Utah 84152
www.izzardink.com

Library of Congress Cataloging-in-Publication Data

Names: Dunn, Jeffrey, 1956- author.

Title: Whiskey rebel / Jeffrey Dunn.

Description: First edition. | Salt Lake City, Utah : Izzard Ink Publishing, 2025.

Identifiers: LCCN 2024054769 (print) | LCCN 2024054770 (ebook) | ISBN 9781642281033 (hardback) | ISBN 9781642281026 (paperback) | ISBN 9781642281040 (ebook) | ISBN 9781642281057 (ebook other)

Subjects: LCGFT: Novels.

Classification: LCC PS3604.U5586 W48 2025 (print) | LCC PS3604.U5586 (ebook) | DDC 813/.6–dc23/eng/20241227

LC record available at https://lccn.loc.gov/2024054769

LC ebook record available at https://lccn.loc.gov/2024054770

Designed by Daniel Lagin
Cover Design by Andrea Ho
Section Images: shutterstock.com/Dmitriy Samorodinov
Back Cover Author Photo: Kelly Tareski
First Edition

Contact the author at info@izzardink.com or inchitensee@gmail.com

Hardback ISBN: 978-1-64228-103-3
Paperback ISBN: 978-1-64228-102-6
eBook ISBN: 978-1-64228-104-0
Audiobook ISBN: 978-1-64228-105-7

With love as beautiful as the Columbia Basin,
this novel is for my son Beck Shepherd
and lifelong friend Bob Fouratt.

CONTENTS

PART TWO
Letting It Slide

PART THREE
Distilling Freedom

Opening Salvos

And did our feet below our spine
tread upon Moses Coulee brown:
And did the sacred skink divine
wear taxless whiskey's sagey crown!

—PUNXIE TAWNEY

Your eyes have seen the glory
of the firin' of the still:
it is cookin' up the sour mash
so the body gets a thrill;
we will loose this fateful lightnin'
'til we've had our spirits' fill:
our whiskey's flowin' on!

Dirty story, barracuda!
Dirty story, barracuda!
Dirty story, barracuda!
Our whiskey's flowin' on!

—HAMILTON CHANCE

PART ONE

❧⟨⟩:⟨⟩❧

The
Whiskey
Rebel

EXPLANATION

I'm from the dark side of the Cascade Mountains, a place where the American Dream sprouts next to the ghost pipe in the rain-drenched woods. Ghost pipe, you ask? Some call it a plant, but it has no chlorophyl and looms as white as my mom's face. She's the one who buried my dad and then followed shortly thereafter. Their story, like our nation's history, is a dark romance. Interested? I'll circle back by and by.

As for folks like me—ones who've grown up under blankets of Cascadian dank shade—coffee wakes us up, and alcohol puts us to sleep. Some say heroin also does the trick. I wouldn't know about that, though I've heard tell. What I can say is that I've seen enough to keep me from looking down the barrel of a needle. I've learned not to judge.

When I was in grade school, there was a guy who split firewood with my dad. Both the man and my dad had their own splitting mauls, and they shared a wedge. The guy also brought his son along, and my dad tasked the boy and me with stacking the woodstove-size pieces. A month later, the guy was cold and fish-eyed. When I asked my dad what happened, he first explained what a coroner was. He then gave me the coroner's verdict, "heroin overdose," but didn't tell me what that meant. I didn't ask. I learned early on that there are different kinds of silence, and one of them advises, "Figure it out yourself."

Later when I was in high school, there was a new kid in my class. My first impression was that he didn't say much and didn't smile at all. I also started seeing him around on his bike. There weren't a lot of streets to ride on—a few on either side of Highway 12—but when a kid needed to get out of the house, there it was. Not long after, the kid disappeared. My dad told me the kid hanged himself with a lamp cord. He said both the kid's parents were heroin addicts, and apparently so was the kid. I understood all I needed to know, the finality of it all.

All that being true, I'm not much interested in the past. I've learned that memories of the dark side don't help. They're just a box of old photographs that remind me the past is really no place to live. After all, although a dark romance may be a romance—a place where a ghost plant is supposed to live—it's not where I want to spend the rest of my life. At least, not if I can help it.

What does interest me is what came *after* I left the dark side of the Cascades, after I left the sun's absence, after I left the supernaturally thick fog, sky-eclipsing steep ridges, and preternaturally tall trees, and after I traveled east over White Pass and into the Columbia Basin, a place where the sun's presence tans a man's skin to lizard leather.

I got the idea to leave my birthplace from a poster hanging in the hallway of my high school, one that said the American Dream started in college. That was news to me. Before that poster, I was told over and over that the American Dream began the day I was born. But my mom, who was the town librarian and who had been to college, said the poster made sense to her and encouraged me to apply. My dad said that college was "bullshit," one of his favorite words. He was a freelance, "gyppo," logger, usually drunk when not on the job, and to him everything was "bullshit." I heard my dad. I listened to my mom.

After a year of community college, my brain was filled with more facts and ideas—I even picked up a skill or two—but none of it felt enlightening. If this were the portal to the American Dream, I couldn't find the light switch. I still felt like I was in the dark.

For a second time, I took the advice of a schoolhouse poster. This one looked me in the eye, jabbed me in the chest, and proclaimed, "Be All You Can Be!" Ah, an action statement straight from the mouth of the American Dream, or so I thought, and I promptly enlisted in America's wrestling match with Iraq.

Naïve? No doubt. Had I asked my mom, she would have sadly smiled as moms do when her son decides to fight down at the local bar or away on a distant battlefield. Had I asked my dad, he would have laughed his sardonic laugh, a chuckle that said, "Boy, there's nothin' like a good ass kickin'."

But I didn't ask, and soon after I was on an all-expenses-paid tour of scenic Anbar Province in the back of a High Mobility Multipurpose Wheeled Vehicle, aka Humvee. There's not a lot to see inside a Humvee: the driver, the guy next to him riding shotgun, the guy next to me in the back, and the blur out the window.

I remember we were talking about girls back home, some of it pretty crude. Then it got quiet. I was probably making up a story in my head—something I do to pass the time. Maybe it was a vision of a girl named Topaz, a hippie chick, and we were at a farmer's market. Her hair was long and sun-kissed. She was wearing cutoff jean shorts and biting into a juicy pear. The juice was running from one corner of her mouth.

I was just about to—

Bang! An improvised explosive device handed me my ass. Rang my bell. Rattled my cage.

I don't really remember the explosion, although I was told later that it was just a garden variety DIY blast. What I do remember, but only vaguely, was that up became down and down became up, and when they pulled me out, down was still up. And when they rolled me onto a stretcher and then later onto an evac hospital bed, someone asked, "What's your name, soldier?" and damned if I didn't know. What's more, damned if I didn't care.

A few weeks later, I returned to the States, and with my brains scrambled like eggs on a breakfast plate, I blasted off again, only this time metaphorically so, rocketing from the Cascade Mountains into the Columbia Basin where the sun's radiation bakes a man's bones to tumbleweed skeleton.

This then is the story of what happened after I touched down, the one that begins with Hamilton Chance, the whiskey rebel who cooked up and distilled the American Whiskey Rebellion of 1794, the first attempt to set America straight. It's also an account of the adventures he and I had, the three other seekers we met along the way, and how the five of us wrestled among ourselves and what came of that wrestling match out in Moses Coulee, the place where, and I swear this to be true, the rattlesnakes lie out in sage leaf bikinis.

PANNING FOR HAMILTON

I saw Hamilton for the first time while panning for gold. I was working a long-ago hot spot down from the Shaser Creek Placer on Peshastin Creek, a nice little run that feeds into the Wenatchee River that feeds the mighty Columbia—all flowing through the sunny-side up of the Cascades.

Standing under a high desert sky, I scooped up a pan full of Peshastin water and gravel. I swished it to the left, back to the right, and again to the left. The rhythm was soothing. The scent of warm ponderosa pine filled the air. I was hoping for some sparkle, a nugget that turned going balls-up in Iraq into just another war story. But when I stopped swishing and looked down at the bottom of my pan, all I saw was gravel. Discouraging, really, so I quit gazing down at all that gravel and looked up to the Old Blewett Pass Road. There I saw a man ambling along, and as he came close, he stopped and shouted down, "You worshippin' the golden calf?"

"Yes, sir! And I think it's a false god at that."

"Come on up. We'll parley."

Depressed and lonely, I tucked my pan into my chocolate chip backpack—Army slang for six-color desert camouflage—and scrambled up the embankment. No, I didn't know this man from the recently departed Saddam Hussein, and, no,

I didn't really care. At this point, what most people call caring had been kicked out of me.

When I reached road grade, the man pulled a smoky glass bottle out of his back pocket and introduced himself. "Hamilton Chance."

"Punxie Tawney," I returned.

The man stood a thin six foot four, not muscular thin but rail thin, a lankiness that suggested some irregularity in his eating habits. His bark-brown hair and curly beard had been trimmed in a self-inflicted scissor-cut, and his feet were bare. He unscrewed the cap of his bottle, kicked back a swig, and offered it saying, "Punxie, huh? Take a hit."

"Yes, sir, Punxie." After taking the bottle, I had a swallow of my own.

"Yep, I like it. Reminds me of where I'm from, way back in Pennsylvania. Where're you headed?"

I handed Hamilton back his bottle and told him about my plans to strike it rich along the Peshastin. I also told him if that didn't work out, I'd try my hand at picking peaches in the Wenatchee fruit fields. And then I told him if that fell flat, I'd be up Olalla Canyon without a neddy, which most folks call a donkey.

"Count me in," Hamilton answered back, "just as long as we don't run into any de Milos."

The True History of Sazerac

Because it's easy to overlook another man's faults when loneliness gnaws the soul, and since my options were the man in front of me, a red harvester ant down at my feet, or a buzzard high above my head, I chose the man who offered me his bottle. I was also curious about something the man said—"just as long as we don't run into any de Milos"—but I saved that question for later.

As we walked along the Old Blewett Pass Road heading toward Washington State 97, we nipped at Hamilton's bottle, and as the bottle went back and forth, I recalled the time my dad told me to pay close attention to what a man drinks. He said it was a window into a man's soul. And then my dad said, "Boy, any man who orders a cheap shot and a beer is off to a good start." If there was one thing my dad understood, it was drinking, so I listened up when Hamilton began to preach on his bottle.

"You see, this ain't just any old bottle. Thing is, this once had rattlesnake oil in it made by The Yaquis Medicine Company of San Francisco, California, and Portland, Oregon. It was *the* genuine article. Just like that"—he snapped his fingers—"it cured any and all your aches and pains."

"Sounds like a pretty good racket."

"Yep, but I can do The Yaquis Medicine Company one better by fillin' this ol' bottle with a Sazerac of my own makin'."

"That's what we're drinking?"

"That we are."

"And what exactly is Sazerac?"

"Curious, I like that. And since you asked, Sazerac has a long and glorious history. All goes back to Louie of the Roaches. He was drinkin' with painters and poets and czars, all them Frenchies, and he told them boys, 'I can do this absence you're

9

drinkin' one better. Here, let me spike it with some whiskey. And then I'll do that one better. I'll sprinkle in some dandelion and mint leaves. Then, I'll add a sugar cube. Now, Vinnie Van G, tell me that don't give you a starry, starry night!' And you know what ol' Louie put in every bottle of Sazerac? A roach, of course. It was his family's totem, so there's always a roach at the bottom of every bottle. It makes it authentatious."

Right off the bat, I thought Hamilton Chance was a tornado twisting inside a kaleidoscope, and my first instinct was to proceed slowly until a suitable exit route appeared. But following close behind was my second instinct, one that told me to follow the intriguing thread running through this man's homespun weave. Sure, some of his word choice was hit or miss, but his replacements weren't pure nonsense. I've been known to say one thing and mean another, so I could see how he switched out *absinthe* for *absence.* And sure, his grasp of history was all over the place. He had Russian czars confused with French kings, and some long-dead Louis chatting up Vincent Van Gogh. And then there was the cockroach thing—I guess he had that confused with the worm in the tequila bottle. But all that aside, I thought it was kind of clever the way he connected his crackpot Sazerac history with Van Gogh's famous painting.

Yes, maybe I should have chosen safety first, but that's not how I was raised. I grew up in the timber town of Packwood, Washington, and my dad worked in the woods falling, bucking, and yarding trees. He was an all-Packwood man, which is to say, if he wasn't out working, he was elk hunting or salmon fishing or drinking, and because of who he was and who he associated with, he kept a long string of characters coming my way.

To be clear, these characters were not the people from whom we get the phrase "men and women of good character." There was nothing upstanding, middle-of-the-road, or church-going—namely respectable—about the folks of Packwood, Washington. I don't recall anyone in Packwood ever being described as "upstanding," and if so, such a person would have been targeted and cut down to size.

The characters I'm talking about were of two types: people who were socially reactive and people who lived singular life-styles. The socially reactive ones were like the old man who sat by himself in the Packwood tavern, and when someone spoke, he hollered something disagreeable across the bar, got up, and started a fight. Or the woman who had driven away husbands, family members, and friends and then moved to Packwood, not to drink at the tavern, but to curl up at home with her BFF bottle of wine. Or the man who built a bomb shelter with his own two hands, moved in, and spent every night on his car battery–powered HAM radio talking up the impending demolition of the world.

I won't go so far to say that my dad was one of these, but there's no doubt that he had an affinity for these sorts of folks. He knew how to talk to them. He sympathized with them. And when he and I were together, he introduced me to them. Over time, I became accustomed to keeping company with those my dad considered his "tribe." These folks' battles were usually personal, but for my dad, it was strictly political. He refused to cut timber for big companies. He talked a lot about the International Workers of the World and used words like "capitalist masters" and "industrial democracy." He often railed against being "thrown out like a discarded machine" and yet never joined the IWW or any other union. Why? Because Logger Bob Tawney simply wasn't a joiner, and although he was a skilled woodsman, he was, at best, a seasonal employee.

And then there were the people who lived singular lifestyles. These characters were never unpleasant and were always easy to talk to, but other people considered them weird. Take the woman whose building was one-third home; one-third barn for chickens, rabbits, and goats; and one-third wildlife refuge. She had a northern spotted owl who nested above her bed and flew out at night only to return in the morning. Or the man who squatted in an abandoned logging company bunkhouse and supported himself by foraging and hiring himself out as an "invasive species" bounty hunter. Or the woman who lived in a tree house and sold sculptures that she made from deadwood and other forest objects.

These singular characters were my mom's folks. As librarian, she catered to them by collecting a complete set of the *Whole Earth Catalog* as well as books on wildlife husbandry, deep ecology, woodcraft, and back-to-nature sculpture. Because our home was too small to satisfy my mom's all-consuming book obsession, the Packwood Library was her first home and our sleeping quarters her second. Furthermore, because my mom was also a distinctive character, being a librarian wasn't enough. She didn't just open up in the morning and lock up at night. She did more than simply check out and shelve books. A few of her folks even called her Pastor Beth and considered the Packwood Library her church, the sanctuary where she offered up readings, heard everyone's confessions, and on rainy days under the fluorescent lights, planned all tomorrows' services.

As for her li'l Punxie, I bopped out the door every morning and headed to school or the woods, but when school was shut and rain was falling, which was a lot of the time, Pastor Beth stuffed me in a rain poncho and whisked me off to her library. Once inside, she peeled off the poncho, sat me next to a window, and handed me a book. At first, I read the usual children's books, but soon I graduated to history accounts, nature guides, and science reports. As I matured, she slipped me Richard Brautigan, who opened my imagination, put a pen in my hand, and started me scribbling my own stories. Next came Jack Kerouac, Jerzy Kosinski, John Irving, and Tom Robbins. My eyes feasted on art and photography books; I never got enough.

All of this goes to explain why I stayed and listened to Hamilton Chance, a man woven from both threads of my upbringing, a man who already seemed to me both reactive and singular, and the man who, right after telling me about Vinnie Van G, went on to say, "And that's only the half of it. All those Frenchies have been livin' in communes since the Romans mixed it up with the Vikings. It's crazy over there. Been that way since caveman times. And all that's right here in that little bottle you're pullin' on. And I'll let you in on my own little secret."

"What's that?"

"Thing is, absence is hard to come by, and even when it comes my way, it's downright expensive. So you know what I do?"

"I can't say that I do."

13

"Instead of absence and a sugar cube, I drop a black licorice gummy bear in a bottle of cheap bourbon. If you're not in a big-ass hurry and wait for the gummy to dissolve, who's to know? Great, huh?"

"It's got a head start," I replied.

"Got a lot of secrets, you know. Got to get by."

Bass Fishing the 97

When Hamilton and I got out to the 97, we turned left and headed north toward Peshastin, a little town on the Wenatchee River. We decided to try our luck at hitchhiking. Our plan was to bum a ride, and when we stopped to look up and down the road, Hamilton said, "You know, hitchhikin's just like bass fishin'."

"Really?"

"Think about it. When I go bass fishin', I start out bluff-burnin', which is workin' down the shoreline. If that ain't the same as hitchin' along the side of the road, I don't know what is."

"That makes sense."

"The way I figure it, we should do our hitchin' like we're bass fishin'."

"Why not. It sounds like it's worth a try."

"First off, let's try dead stickin'. Now, cast out your thumb and hold it there steady-like. Keep it simple."

We watched the cars pass for a while until Hamilton said, "Nah, need some drama. Pitch skippin's just the thing, and for that just cast out your thumb and bounce it along as you go."

"You mean, like this?"

"Yep, like that."

The cars came and the trucks went, but we were just a couple of fence posts to them. "Sheee-it! Better pull out the big gun, walkin' the dog. Now, cast out that thumb of yours, and when it's way out, and I mean way-ay-ay out, jig it back to the left and back to the right and back to the left and back to the right. Got to give them a show they cain't refuse."

Unfortunately, nothing our thumbs did got us down the road. "I hate to say it, Hamilton, but it looks like the foot is mightier than the thumb."

"Sheee-it, Punxie. That's the sorry truth. Don't like takin' no for an answer—no way, no how—but a man's got to do what a man's got to do."

STILL LIFE ON HAMILTON

Hamilton and I really didn't get very far down the 97. We only traveled a mile or so, because after 1,760 steps—Hamilton was the one who counted—we stopped, looked up at a sign that read "BLEWETT," and Hamilton said, "Punxie, it's a sign."

"Yes, sir, I can see that."

"Need to listen to the oracle."

"And what does it say, Hamilton?"

"Leave no roadside attraction unexplored."

Following Hamilton's maxim, we went off-road and poked around Blewett, which turned out to be nothing more than some mining ruins, and after we got tired of that, we hauled up on an old stamp mill timber, the leftover support beam of a contraption that bygone miners used to crush ore.

"The way I see it," Hamilton said, pointing at an unnamed wash just below, "a boy came up this very creek. You see, he'd lost the twinkle in his eye back when good-time Lucy upped her prices, so he stuck in his pan, swish, swish, swish, and '*eureka, oh shit, and a good goddamn,*' the sparkle at the bottom of his pan put the twinkle right back in his eye."

As I listened to Hamilton, he began to sound a lot like Dean Moriarity in *On the Road* or Lee Mellon in *A Confederate General on the Big Sur* or Plucky Purcell in *Another Roadside Attraction*. And while my mind was wandering somewhere between flesh-and-blood people and paper-and-ink characters, I wondered what was up with Hamilton's bare feet. Normally, what a man does or doesn't wear isn't any concern of mine, but seeing as there was a lull in the conversation, I took a crack at satisfying my curiosity.

"I see you lost your shoes."

"Lost?" Hamilton questioned back. "Nah, just keepin' my soles stuck to this earth. You follow?"

"Yes, sir. Maybe you should paint your feet and call them a still life," I replied, imagining Hamilton's feet looking something like Van Gogh's *Shoes*, a painting I saw in an art book in my mom's library.

"Yep, wouldn't that be somethin'? Still life . . . hmm. I like that. I'll tell you somethin' else. Sometimes I like to put my Sazerac bottle between my naked feet, roll back like the yogis in Jellystone Park, and drink. Then, I'm the circle of life, Punxie. The circle of life."

Bobbi Lee Chance

After expanding on the topic of his bare feet, Hamilton shifted back to telling me about his roots. He wanted me to know all about his great-great-great-grandfather, one Bobbi Lee Chance, a man who fought for liberty during the Whiskey Rebellion, a long-forgotten time when Western Pennsylvania's Mingo Creek was threatened by the British to the north, by the Seneca and Shawnee to the west, by the Spanish from the south, and by George Washington to the east. A time when baby-faced America betrayed its Boston Tea Party roots by taxing whiskey to support a standing army, a military force that in 1794 was used against the very folks who stuffed its stomach.

"Yep, Bobbi Lee Chance, he was somethin'. He fired up the first still on Mingo Creek and took on the exciseman. The story goes he prayed to a whiskey barrel Mary. You know, just like the bathtub Marys you see in people's backyards."

"Sorry, I don't think I'm familiar."

"No? Well, let me tell you. Back where I'm from, folks take an old bathtub, tip it straight up, bury it halfway down, and then put a Mary statue in it. I like to think Bobbi Lee Chance did the same thing, except he split a whiskey barrel longwise and buried that instead of a bathtub."

"Very inspirational."

"That it is, Punxie. I plan to follow in the whiskey rebel footsteps of my three-times great-granpappy and start a revolution."

"A revolution? What *exactly* are you fighting for?"

"Thing is, it's personal. I'm not the great-great-great-grandson of Bobbi Lee Chance for nothin'. Why, I'm the only child of the Whiskey Rebellion not-at-all removed. I got the Whiskey Rebellion jaw, and the Whiskey Rebellion tongue, and the Whiskey Rebellion lower lip. I'm tellin' you, the Whiskey Rebellion and me spoon every night."

"Yes, sir. I understand how you feel. It's a family thing, your legacy and all that, but you said you had a plan?"

"First off, Punxie, I'm settin' up a still. And it's not goin' to be just any old still, not by a long shot, because it's goin' to be of the tax-free variety. Just think about it. Why, together, *we* could start cookin' up our forefathers' whiskey."

We? Together? I reverted back to my first instinct, the one where I grab a life preserver and jump ship. It wasn't because I was against revolutions on principle—after all, every Fourth of July America lights its fuse with alcohol-fueled war hoops and sets the sky ablaze—but in Iraq I saw firsthand what happens to insurgents.

Then my second instinct kicked in, the one where I became intrigued by the idea of going into the whiskey business. It's not like Hamilton mentioned Oklahoma City, or even Ruby Ridge. Maybe he was only interested in free enterprise with an emphasis on *free*. I had no argument with that. I didn't see any reason not to let events play out, at least in the short term. I've heard there is a thin line between crazy and genius, and I didn't want to kick myself later if Hamilton beat the odds.

My Turn

We slept out under the Peshastin Creek stars like a couple of gold diggers panning for the American Dream, and a few hours into our sleep, the sun came up through the ponderosa pines—a warm sun, a tenderhearted mother of a sun—satisfying like a first helping of oatmeal on a spring morning.

"Hey, Punxie, what about you? Not every day I meet a fellow whiskey rebel."

"No, Hamilton, I don't suppose you do." And there it was again, "whiskey rebel." Like I said, "whiskey rebel" wasn't a road I wanted to go down, but "whiskey entrepreneur"? Sure, I was listening. So rather than throw the beautiful girl out with the bathwater, I went on to tell Hamilton about my first day of school, the time when, right off the bat, I didn't like my teacher. I remembered that she had on a red fright wig, and being who I was, when she turned her back, I picked up, ran straight out the door, and didn't stop until I got to my mom's library.

"Sheee-it, Punxie! I knew you were a freedom fighter."

That gave me a smile, and I went on and told Hamilton about growing up off the 12 in Packwood, Washington, about my logger dad and librarian mom, and about how as a child I was either loose in the woods or lost in a book. I told him I tried my hand at writing stories and had some fun with girls, and when I graduated from White Pass High School, I made a pilgrimage to college, but after a year, I'd had enough of school, joined the Army, and got my ass shipped to Iraq where my ass went *boom* all the way back to the States.

"Boom, huh? Damn, brother."

"*Bah boom* as I remember it. While I was in the evac hospital, I found out my dad was dead. And back home in a vet hospital, I found out my mom was dead. After all that, I was loose in the woods again, and when I was drinking in a bar, this old-timer told me about a place called the Peshastin Creek Placer. I figured I'd come up here. Maybe it would pay off. I'd never been on this side of the Cascades, but I didn't have anything else going on. I figured it was worth a try."

"Then you saw me."

"Yes, sir. And then I saw you."

PRELUDE TO CARDS ON THE TABLE

Because my stomach was waking up, I stopped talking and began to rummage through my backpack. I thought a few granola bars would do the trick, and when I found a couple, I offered one to Hamilton, tore the wrapper off another, and then we both went to eating and conversing some more.

"You're a long way from Pennsylvania," I said. "Isn't that where you said you're from?"

"Mingo Creek. Southwest Pennsylvania. West Appalachia foothills. You know about it?"

"I have a general idea. Not exactly, of course, but Pennsylvania's sort of like here. Got an east side, west side thing going on with mountains in the middle, right?"

"Yep."

"But I'm curious—and shoot me down if I'm patrolling a sensitive area—how'd you get from there to here?"

"Freedom, brother."

"Understood, but how did you get from one side of the Rockies to the other?"

"You got an inquiring mind, Punxie. Once you sink your teeth in, you don't let go, so here's something you don't know.

You see, you had parents—sorry they're gone—but I didn't. Sheee-it! I had a mom and a dad but don't recall meetin' 'em. My granpappy, he was it. We had a trailer. Food. Mattress on the floor. Never hit me, and I never hit him. We were good most of the time."

"Did you ever find out about what happened with your parents?"

"Nah, never talked about it. Course, I asked, but my granpappy just tickled me. When I was older, he didn't do that—too big. He just said, 'Hammy, get the hell out and chase squirrels.' Then he'd smile. Always smiled."

"I think I get it. My dad was good at changing the subject too. I never figured out why he didn't answer a lot of my questions. Oh, he was full of advice and stories, but when it came to my questions, he talked about everything but the answers. He was a mystery sometimes. But hey, I still want to know why you hoofed it out of Mingo Creek."

"'Hoofed it out,' that's good. There's some gold in that pan of yours, Punxie, but Mingo Creek? Why'd I leave? Thing is, I like to drum, loved to ever since I was a kid. I was always banging on things. Whenever I'd get all hyped up, I go to bangin', and the more regular the bangin', the calmer I got. Course, bangin' on things don't always go over well. Take school, for example. Me and school didn't get along. Played in the school band but couldn't do band all day. You know how it is."

"Yes, sir. I think I do."

"And then granpappy died, and right after that, me and school parted ways. Kicked around a while, drifted from there to here, from Mingo Creek to Louisville, Kentucky, and then along the Natchez Trace from Nashville, Tennessee, to Tupelo, Mississippi, all the way to New Orleans. Started out with a construction bucket and an ice cream container and a paint can with pennies on top and made money layin' down some skiffle. My best setup was in New Orleans' Pirate Alley where I worked the tourists. Some folks said my groove was Sigsbee Deep, which if you don't know is at the bottom of the Gulf of Mexico."

"I've never been to New Orleans, but I've heard it's a musical place."

"Oh, it is. I'd set up my kit and then call to my flock. Start them out with something like, 'Ladies and gents, whores and hobos, gather 'round while I hatch some swamp stomp. My ghost notes will foreplay, slay, and convey 'til you ascend to transcend, never to reoffend.' "

"You must've attracted quite a crowd."

"Oh, I did."

"So why'd you leave New Orleans?"

"You see, one night just before I left town, this young couple got caught in my sweet spot, and they began to groove, and their eyes caught the flaming tongues of a dying sun, so I went deeper. Not louder, *deeper*. And I started to reel that young couple in, and I called out, 'Hey, why don't you two hop on my little voodoo rhythm ship? Give you some sultry funk lessons and all my good looks for a floor to curl up on. Deal?' And you know what the guy said, Punxie?"

"No, sir, I don't"

"Why, he said, 'Deal.' And that young gal? Well, she just smiled."

"Then what happened?"

"What happened was, we walked all the way from Pirate Alley to Arabi, and let me tell you, Arabi's one spooky place. I been told it's all watched over by the ghosts of slaughtered animals and people who burned down the courthouse."

"It's not for the faint of heart, I take it."

"Nah, certainly not, not by half. Finally, we came to this broken-down shotgun shack. The young gal said she'd inherited it from her grandma, and after she opened the door, the guy said all whiney like, 'Okay, now you got to play somethin' I can follow,' and I told him, 'Nah, you cain't follow me because you don't got my time feel.' But he wouldn't stop whinin', 'Come on! Let me follow,' but I just kept tellin' him, 'Nah, man, you too much in the meat-world.' "

"But what about the girl?"

"I'm gettin' to that. You see, I was after two things. First, I don't like sleepin' out in a city. Oh, I'm partial to outside like this. Coyotes and bears, they're nothin', but in the city, I can do without the carniwhores—know what I mean—so I was aimin' to get under a roof. Also, I hoped to snag me some bus fare out, but that young gal had other ideas. Not that I minded. Got to give a little to get a little, you know? So she dragged me by the hand through the kitchen and into the bedroom, and after she slammed the door, she threw me down on the bed and said to me, 'You ever see the movie *Jules et Jim*? Let's play. You're Jim. I'm Kate.' "

"I've never heard of it. *Jules et Jim*, you say? Have you seen it?"

"Nah, but that was none of my concern because I lay on that bed and said to her, 'Bus fare,' and she just blinked at me, so I spelled it out. 'I need two hundred fifty dollars or I'm goin' to tell your boyfriend that you got a thing for threesomes.' And you know what she said back?"

"Go on." I really wanted to know.

"She said, 'Maybe Jules would like that.' And I said, 'Sheee-it! I don't know about any Jules,' and she said somethin' like, 'Spittle, dee-dee, kind sir. It seems you like a girl with a healthy overbite.' I wanted her to stick to the point, so I said, 'Am I get-tin' my bus fare?' And she said, 'Of course, as long as I get to have my fun.'"

"And then?"

"And then I said to her, 'Suit yourself.' And she said, 'You're sexy, a regular Venus de Milo,' and went about havin' her fun."

"Did you get your money?"

"I'm here, ain't I?" Hamilton smiled, putting his crooked teeth on full display. "Cain't be free in a city, too many people. In the morning, I pinched the guy on the ass and gave the gal some tongue and walked out the door. And you know what else, Punxie?"

"There's more?"

"The air was so muddy I passed a humpback blue catfish going the other way. Took it as a sign."

"And what did the catfish say?"

"To go as far as that two hundred and fifty would take me."

"Which ended up being Wenatchee?"

"Yep, and then I heard something about gold, so I hitched up into these mountains."

The Real American Salesman

When Hamilton was done revealing why he didn't want to see any de Milos in the Peshastin Drainage, I asked him if he wanted to go back to North Sasher Creek, pan for gold, and strike it rich, but he said, "Nah."

Then I asked if he wanted to go farther up into the mountains. Or maybe he wanted to pitch in with the migrants in some agricultural baron's red delicious apple orchard. Or if push came to shove, he might want to go down Peshastin Creek, down the Wenatchee River, and down the Columbia scouting for hippie chicks. Maybe some earth mommas would take pity on us and propose we start a commune, nothing to do but enjoy the fruits of their femininity. And to all this he said, "Nah, Punxie, need to keep all my channels open."

"Well, what then?"

"Go prospectin' for Bobbi Lee."

"How's that?"

"My orangin' story. You know, my three-times great-granpappy Bobbi Lee Chance and the Whiskey Rebellion. Me and you need to be pannin' the Wenatchee Public Library."

"Are you sure?" I didn't think Hamilton was the library-researching type.

"Does the heads kick like a mule?"

"Come again?"

"The heads, brother, the heads. First part of the distillin' wash is mostly alcohol. But it's okay. You got a lot to learn, that's all."

"Yes, sir, that's for certain," I said, and it was settled. Our destination was the Wenatchee Public Library. What could go wrong? I mean, it's a library, right?

Soon, we were back to thumb fishing, but this time the cars were biting because right away we snagged a salesman driving a rusted-out, primer-gray Chevelle SS. "Where you two headed?"

"Wenatchee."

"Hop in, boys. I can take you as far as Highway 2. You'll need to find another ride because I'm going the other way to Leavenworth and then on to Gold Bar. You need any knives? I've got some in my trunk. My name's Gus Badelli, and I sell Chop Inc. cutlery. I can get you boys clearance on a *kiritsuke*. That knife will make you a real teppanyaki maestro. The ladies like that sort of thing. It'll get you past her shoji screen, if you know what I mean."

He was a real American salesman, free to roam from place to place pitching his wares. And while I sat in the back seat—Hamilton was the one riding shotgun—it occurred to me that I got my ass blown up so that the guy in the rearview mirror with the slicked-back hair could sit in a motel bar tonight, wait for the last call, and offer his room key to the only woman still in the place.

Was I angry? Sure, the kind of anger lots of veterans—ones who have seen some action—have when they return home. But I had trouble placing my anger. Right off, I didn't like the guy. But why? Wrong generation? Wrong fashion sense? Wrong vibe? Maybe it wasn't so much him. Maybe I was angry at the images emerging in my mind, one where the equestrian statue of Lieutenant George Washington had slicked-back hair, and another one where the Statue of Liberty had slicked-back hair, and finally the one where the soldiers lifting the flag on the Iwo Jima Memorial had slicked-back hair.

But my mom taught me to be polite, so I put those images out of my head, the one rattled by Iraqi insurgents not so long ago, and answered the man's question: "No, Mr. Badelli. I can't say we need any knives."

ℬRIGITTE ℬARDOT

When the 97 ended about five miles down the road, the salesman dropped us off, and we started thumb fishing the 2. Fortunately, the cars were still biting because no sooner had we done a bit of pitch skipping, then down off the mountain came a cherry-red Italian sports car. The driver was a blonde who had her hands on a rattlesnake-skin-covered steering wheel. Her hair and scarf blew back like Brigette Bardot's in a movie magazine photo, one that I'd seen in the Packwood Public Library.

After she pulled off the road, we trotted up to the passenger side, and Hamilton asked, "Headin' to Wenatchee?"

"What business you two got in Wenatchee?" she questioned back.

"Hittin' up the Wentachee Public Library," Hamilton continued.

"You two? Reading? Not much chance of that."

"You got us all wrong. We're headin' there for some serious historical research," Hamilton objected.

"Is that right?"

"Yes, ma'am," I chimed in, although I wasn't much interested in talking. I really was more interested in looking. There was so much to see. Her oversize sunglasses. Her pouty lips.

"Tell me, what's it like, this reading you two are doing?"

"Thing is, me and him—that's Punxie here, and I'm Hamilton, pleased to meet you—we're hittin' up the library because me and my buddy are goin' to dig into the soil of my roots. You see, I'm descended from *the* Bobbi Lee Chance."

"My goodness, I've never heard of Bobbi Lee. What did you say his last name was?"

"Chance."

"Chance . . . right. Bobbi Lee Chance. No, I've never heard of your relative, but since this is all about family, you two hop in. By the by, my name's Michelle Beaverton Justice, and since I'm heading through town anyway, the Wenatchee Public Library it is."

Because my policy is never to say no to a woman, especially one who wants to take me for a ride, I opened the passenger door, flipped the front seat forward, and plopped my butt down on the hard back bench. Not to be outdone, Hamilton clicked shut the car door, deftly vaulted over the side, and stuck the landing. The lady? She didn't even flinch. Her only reaction to Hamilton's butt cheeks hitting her bucket seat was to pop the clutch and peel us out onto the 2's downslope.

From where I was sitting, I could see Hamilton's lips flapping and our young beauty's head bobbing. Unfortunately, I couldn't engage in the conversation—too much wind—so I just sat back and savored the desert browns broken by the irrigated greens. I also appreciated the road signs. On the right was "BO-PEEP APPLES" and then came "SKOOKUM PEACHES." And to the left was:

KETCHUP

WITH

JESUS

LETTUCE PRAISE

& RELISH HIM

'CUZ HE LOVES ME

FROM MY HEAD

TO-MA-TOES

Relaxing, I enjoyed the pull of the little sportscar as it hugged the hillsides and caressed the riverbanks. But after a downshift, all the soft curves were replaced by hard, straight lines. Motel railings. Parking lot lines. In-N-Out window frames. Supermarket rows. Bench slats. Telephone pole erections. Three-dollar, twenty-seven cents a gallon gas stations.

We passed a mom pushing a rattle-wheeled baby carriage. Her toddler desperately gripped her index finger. A rheumy-eyed dog panted from inside the stroller. In the background was a congregation of migrant men. They must have missed the work truck, or maybe the work truck never came.

I felt a jerk. We pulled a hard right and a hard left, and the vehicle slid tight against the curb, the one on the passenger side and in front of the Wenatchee Public Library.

"Welcome to Wenatchee, boys."

Hamilton responded by opening the door and spilling sunny-side up onto the frying-pan sidewalk. I folded the passenger seat down and tumbled out over-easy. And without so much as a goodbye, Miss Michelle zoomed off, the car's motion clanking the passenger door shut.

"She's somethin', Punxie, a real barracuda in somebody's fishpond. Nah, don't got time for that."

"I think I could make time—under different circumstances, of course."

"Yep, maybe you could, but right now we're goin' to learn a thing or two about Bobbi Lee Chance and the Whiskey Rebellion."

"Yes, sir. That's the plan."

MEETING COYOTE

On the way into the Wenatchee Public Library, we met a coyote sitting on the entrance steps. No, he wasn't a real coyote. Instead, this coyote was a statue of a coyote's head on a life-size human body. Beneath the statue was an information plaque with the artist's name, Rich Beyer, and the statue's name, "Coyote Reads a Candy Wrapper." The artist had dressed up the statue in pants and a rumpled work shirt, the cuffs loosely turned back at the sleeves. The statue also sported a hangman's noose and wore the cheap sandals that some call thongs and others call flip-flops.

I thought that the statue was really something, very life-like and whimsical and disturbing in that double-take sort of way. After a while, I wanted to say, "Hey, Coyote, I'm a big fan. I know you speak to the tribal folks around here, but I also feel like you speak to all of us who lay out under the endless expanse of stars. And you know, Coyote, I think I get that hangman's noose of a necktie you got on because I've got this suspicion that dreams, at least for folks like us, no longer come true. Is that right, Coyote? Is that what that candy wrapper says?"

I wanted to say all that, but I didn't. And just as quietly as we stopped, Hamilton and I silently passed by and opened the door into the Wenatchee Public Library.

THE WENATCHEE LIBRARIAN CHASTITY BELT

"Don't like this place," Hamilton said.

"What do you mean, you don't like this place?"

"Just what I said, don't like this place. Feels like demons cuttin' out a man's soul and splittin' it between Sesamese twins."

"Ah, come on. It's not so bad. A bit sterile, I'll give you that, but we need to meet Bobbi Lee Chance."

"That we do, brother. That we do."

Having dealt with Hamilton's sudden horrors—clearly, he was sensitive in the way a lot of my dad's folks were sensitive—we ventured farther into the library, which for me was like a 1950s airport, more horizontals than verticals. Maybe what was bothering Hamilton was the way the flesh had been stripped from the ceiling's skeleton. There was nothing natural about it. Luckily, the circulation desk had the curves of a naked young woman, one that was lying there just for me. And since we didn't come here to let our imaginations get the best of us, I stepped up and said, "Hi, we're new here."

The woman behind the desk smiled the kind of smile that gave her time to size us up, and I'm pretty sure she had her doubts. She wore a very official-looking lanyard with a very official-looking ID card, which I suspected was also the key to her chastity belt, a device that could only be opened by monks who copied out manuscripts and had taken vows of celibacy.

"Do you have a library card?" she asked. She was good at hiding her suspicions. Good, but not great.

"Well, no," I said.

"Would you like to get one?"

"Sure, if that would help us get along."

"I need a picture ID and some proof of your current address."

"What you're saying, then, is that if we're homeless, we can't be friends?"

The word "friends" made her wince, but she stayed professional and answered my question. "Not necessarily. I can sign you up for an e-card. You can't check out books, but you can use our resources while you are in the building or online."

"Well, sure," I offered.

"Name?"

"Punxie."

"First or last?"

"First."

"Last name."

"Tawney."

"Punxie *Tawney*?"

"Yes, ma'am, Tawney."

"*Punxie* Tawney?"

"Yes, ma'am. I admit it's curious. My last name's Tawney, and my parents, well, they thought it was funny. You know, Groundhog Day and all."

"I see. I'll just type your name in here. Do you have an address?"

"No."

"I see. I do need to put in a city, zip code, and email address."

"What do you think, Hamilton?" I was hoping he could tell me where we lived.

"How about Peshastin, nine eight eight four seven. I saw it on the post office."

"Email?"

"Whiskey rebel at pay no taxes dot rye."

"*R-y-e*?" She narrowed her eyes.

"We're on the booze web," Hamilton smiled sweetly.

"I suppose that will do," she said curtly.

But I wasn't so sure it would do, at least that's not what her lips said, the way they were curled under, the way her teeth bit into them. All the same, I was glad she didn't notice that Hamilton wasn't wearing shoes.

When she finished typing, she said, "Okay, that completes the process. You are welcome to use our resources." She touched her ID badge like a time-trusted diaphragm that she kept near her heart to ward off impregnation.

"Don't think she likes us," Hamilton said in a loud whisper as we moved out of the slack water and into the library's current.

CARDS ON THE TABLE

The first place we headed was the card catalog. After pulling out the drawer labeled *W*, I flipped through the cards and, after finding nothing of use, Hamilton exclaimed, "Sheee-it! This shithole of a library doesn't have a single book on the Whiskey Rebellion! I'm tellin' you, Punxie, it's not American!"

"We're in a library, Hamilton. We need to keep our voices down."

"Down, you say? Down? I'll tell you what's down, Punxie! I'm goin' to burn this den of irritability down!" His voice got louder with each word.

There I was, biding my time for companionship and entertainment purposes, and Hamilton was creating a ruckus. It was like sitting down to a poker game—bets are made, cards are dealt—and suddenly I had to decide if I was in or out. It was like Hamilton had called my hand.

Decisions like these are never brain decisions. They're gut decisions, like the ones made in the guts of every cougar before it attacks or slinks away. As for me, my guts were really sizing Hamilton up, and my mom and dad were the measuring sticks. Yes, Hamilton was like my dad: the alcohol, the confrontational individuality, the talk of revolution. If Hamilton were my dad, I would be out. But Hamilton was also like my mom:

the sociability, the all-consuming vision, the devotion to a cause. If Hamilton were my mom, I was in.

All of this must have been churning inside me because as I led Hamilton away from the card catalog, I asked, "Just to be clear, we're here to find out about the Whiskey Rebellion, right?"

"And my three-times great-grandpappy, don't forget."

"Yes, sir. Him too. But I'm still not clear on your plans—for later, I mean."

"Plans? Make tax-free whiskey, Punxie, just like my granpappy and their granpappies before 'em."

"What about the rebellion stuff?"

Hamilton gave me a quizzical look. "Rebellion stuff?" It was like he'd never considered the word *rebellion* cut loose from the word *whiskey*.

"Do you got a gun, Hamilton? Are there going to be bombs involved? Are you thinking along the lines of Harper's Ferry? You planning on going down in a blaze of lead like Bonnie and Clyde?"

"Nah, Punxie, nothin' like that," Hamilton said, breaking eye contact and pawing the carpet with his foot. "Nah, just want to make whiskey and bottle it and sell it until I meet my granpappy in the sky."

"So you're not talking about real rebellion, the kind that's got guns and bombs?"

"Nah." He looked like a puppy who got caught peeing on the carpet. "Don't got it in me, Punxie. Thing is, guns . . . well they scare me. And bombs? Sheee-it! Never crossed my mind."

"Okay, but where am I in all this?"

"Why you're my fellow whiskey reb— Nah, what's the word? Somebody who makes whiskey and sells it."

"Entrepreneur?"

"Ent— entre—" He stopped trying. "Yep, that word."

"I'd be your whiskey business partner? Is that what you're saying?"

"Sheee-it, brother, that's all I'm sayin'."

"And finding out about the whiskey rebellion and your three-times great-grandfather, that's just research for setting up the business, right?"

"Yep, you'd be a loyal patriot to the whiskey reb—" He cut himself off again. "Sorry, Punxie, did it again. A loyal patriot to the tax-free whiskey cause. You'd be an inspiration and an aberration."

This was the moment my guts decided that Hamilton wasn't like my dad. At least that's how I must've felt. I'd learned that Hamilton was afraid of guns, and I knew that my dad slept with a loaded .357 magnum on his nightstand. And while it seemed like Hamilton's Whiskey Rebellion was code for *free enterprise*, Logger Bob Tawney's alcohol-fueled rebellion was class warfare, or so he preached, at least until a widow maker of tree limb put a stopper in his bottle of talk.

My guts also must've felt that Hamilton was like my mom. Both Hamilton and my mom loved one thing above all else. He treasured homemade spirits, and she worshipped books. And both Hamilton and my mom lived to share their singular passion with the world. Hamilton dreamed that his still would someday be a shrine, and my mom had lived her dream as Pastor Beth of Our Lady of Perpetual Bronte, at least until she locked up for good after my dad died.

All this explains why, instead of turning on my heel and walking away, my next words were, "Hey, Hamilton, I could use a sit-down. Take a load off. Relax a bit. We could do that over there at that open computer. I'll bet we can find the Whiskey Rebellion on the internet too. What do you say to that?"

"Lead the way, brother Punxie, but I don't like it. How do we know it ain't radiospastic?"

"Trust me, Hamilton. I may not know anything about the Whiskey Rebellion, and I sure don't know anything about making whiskey, but I learned a thing or two about computer research from my mom and in college."

"If you say so." Hamilton's smile reassured me that his anxieties were, at least for now, in the past. "We whiskey patriots got to stick together."

Once we were seated, me in the driver's seat and Hamilton riding shotgun, I gazed intently into the computer's jury-rigged TV screen, typed in some search words, and up came a list of links. I then typed in more search words and up came more links. Suddenly—*shazam!*—we hit upon the motherload: *Incidents of the Insurrection in Western Parts of Pennsylvania in the Year 1794*, a book published in 1795 by Hugh Brackenridge, a witness to all the rebellious shenanigans. When I clicked on the link, a download slowly ensued, and finally *Incidents of the Insurrection* appeared, a digital scan of a book written two hundred years before Hamilton and I were born.

Scroll and scan, scroll and scan, scroll and scan. Then after a few minutes, I started skimming a promising block of text. When I stopped, I said louder than I intended, "Look right here, Hamilton! It's a whiskey rebel call to action!"

The Circular Letter
Canonsburgh, 28 July, 1794

Sir,

Having had suspicions that the Pittsburgh post would carry with him the sentiments of some of the people in the country, respecting our present alarming situation; and the letters by the post being now in our possession, by which certain secrets are discovered, hostile to our interest it is therefore now come to that crisis, that every citizen must express his sentiments, not by his words but by his actions. You are then called upon, as a citizen of the western country, to render your personal service, with as many volunteers as you can raise, to rendezvous at your usual place of meeting on Wednesday next; and from there you will march to the usual place of rendezvous at Braddock's fields on the Monongahela on Friday, the first day of August next; to be there at two o'clock in the afternoon, with arms and accoutrements in good order. If any volunteer should want arms and ammunition, bring them forward, and they shall he supplied as well as possible.—Here, sir, is an expedition proposed, in which you will have an opportunity of displaying your military talents, and of rendering service to your country.—Four days provision will be wanted; let the men be well supplied.

We are, &c.

J. Canon,

B. Parkinson,

D. Bradford,

A. Fulton,

T. Speers,

J. Locyhry,

J. Marshall

"Sheee-it, Punxie, look at those names. Why, it's signed in the blood of my ancestors. Glory be to Braddock's Fields, to the Monongahela, and to the holy accoutrements!"

"A sacred book to be sure, Hamilton."

"Keep on goin', Punxie. Got to be more. Just got to be."

Fueled by the battle plans of the Whiskey Rebellion, we went back to scrolling and scanning, and a little while later we hit paydirt again: a document all about the Mingo Meeting House. Here, we stopped and read about the whiskey rebels gathering to keep our new country on course. We learned about the four Pennsylvania and two Virginia counties who were pledged

to meet, and chuse [sic], not more than five, nor less than two, representatives, to meet at Parkinson's ferry, on the Monongahela, on Thursday, the 14th day of August next, to take into consideration the situation of the western country.

It was all very exciting, really. Certainly nothing like what I learned in high school, teachings that felt less like history and more like a recruiting poster for getting my ass kicked.

"You see, I told you about Mingo Creek, Punxie, the blessed stream of my birth. This here's an inspiration. This here gives me faith. Yep, it's just like old Bennie Frankly said, 'Upon these words we'll cook our mash!' "

Tom the Tinker

Now that Hamilton and I had a few gold nuggets at the bottom of our pan, we went back to washing through more digital deposits. It didn't take long for the largest nugget of them all to make an appearance, one reprinted from the *Pittsburgh Gazette* way back in 1794.

In taking a survey of the troops under my command, in the late expedition against that insolent exciseman, John Neville, I find there were a great many delinquents, even amongst those who carry on distilling. It will therefore be observed, that Tom the Tinker will not suffer any certain class, or set of men, to be excluded the service of this my district, when notified to attend on any expedition, in order to obstruct the execution of the law, and obtain repeal thereof.

And I do declare, upon my solemn word, that, if such delinquents do not come forth, on the next alarm, in equipments, and give assistance, as in them lies, in opposing the execution, and obtaining repeal, of the excise law, he, or they, will be deemed as enemies, and standing opposed to the virtuous principles of republican liberty, and shall receive punishment according to the nature of the offense; and that, at least, consumption of his distillery.

Tom the Tinker

"You see, Punxie, it's just like I said. It's the excise. Why, it's the very crusts of the matter. Right here, Tom talks about getting the patriots to go after that tax collector, John Neville. But sheee-it! It also says there was a bunch of traitors who didn't show up to support the cause."

"Yes, sir, that's exactly what it says. Then Tom the Tinker says he's going to sound the alarm to see who shows up again and is ready to fight the whiskey tax. It's a loyalty test, plain and simple."

"You got that right. And I love the punishment, Punxie. The patriots are going to drink up the no-shows' whiskey. Punishment fits the crime. Ain't that right, brother?"

"Roger that."

"And I got to say, Punxie, it's not the first time I've come across these Nevilles. Thing is, my granpappy told me all manner of things about these rascals, including that it was a Neville who set upon my three-times great-granpappy Bobbi Lee, but I've never seen it all laid out so bald face like this."

"That's something, Hamilton. I knew that the Whiskey Rebellion was a big deal to you, but I didn't know your grandfather knew about the bad guy."

"Like I said, Punxie, it's personal." Hamilton then nodded toward the computer screen, and we continued.

Fully charged, I went back to scrolling and scanning, and before long we discovered that this radical Tom the Tinker was possibly more than one man. We also learned that these radical Toms wrote intimidating letters to the sellouts who had registered their stills and paid the whiskey excise tax. Furthermore, these Toms persuaded local newspapers to publish menacing editorials and raised liberty poles with flags that read "Liberty, no excise" and "No asylum for traitors," the folks who supported the tax. We even solved the mystery as to why Tom was called "the tinker." As it turned out, Tom was the one who not only visited the sellouts but also "tinkered" the sellouts' stills into a pile of useless trash. Now that made Hamilton and me laugh because if that wasn't putting your whiskey where your mouth was, we didn't know what was.

"Got to say, Punxie, this Tom the Tinker's not Bobbi Lee Chance, but he's the next best thing."

"And who's to say, Hamilton, that Bobbi Lee wasn't Tom the Tinker? Seems to me we're talking about the two of them with the same breath. I mean, who's to say you're not descended from Tom the Tinker?"

"Sheee-it, I like the way you think. I really do, Punxie, but there's just one more thing that's spoilin' my mash."

"And what's that, Hamilton?"

"You know how they say that before a fight you'd better know your enemy?"

"I think I see where you're headed."

"I think you do, brother. Yep, I think you do."

JOHN NEVILLE

I had to admit this was getting interesting. I mean, it was very American, what with the freedom fighters and the taxation issue, but here the rebels weren't standing in opposition against King George. No, these freedom fighters were rising in defiance of President Washington, the guy I knew from the one-dollar bill. Clearly, the seed of divided loyalty was already planted way back in America's infancy, a seed that also got planted in me when I got flipped on my head in Iraq.

Besides all that, I like a good story. Who was this John Neville? To be sure, he was the bad guy, at least from Hamilton's point of view, and it was only natural that I'd want to know about both the good guy and the bad guy. In my experience, the bad guy was often more interesting.

All that was enough to set me to scrolling and scanning for the "insolent exciseman, John Neville." And since Neville, as some say, was the wadding behind the Whiskey Rebellion's ball, it didn't take long before "John Neville" fired out the barrel.

"Knew it. Just knew it, Punxie. My granpappy might've been full of shit, but sometimes his shit was the starter for some furious compost."

"Yes, sir. I'd say your grandfather was on to something. Now, look right here, Hamilton. All this is pretty dramatic."

The scene started with the whiskey rebels marching on John Neville's house and demanding that Neville, who had been appointed inspector over the whiskey excise, give up his written records. When Neville refused, the rebels demanded that six of their band be let in to take the records. Neville refused again. Then the rebels told Neville that his wife and any other women in the house would be given time to get out before an attack, and after the allotted time, the assault on Neville's house began.

Hamilton and I went on to read about muskets being fired, participants being wounded, and Militia Major James McFarlane—the one in charge of the whiskey rebels—being killed. McFarlane's death was a big deal because he was described as one

> who had served with reputation, in the rank of a lieutenant, in the war with Great Britain, from the beginning to the end of it; and was a man of good private character; and had acquired a very handsome property, by industry in trade, after the expiration of the war.

But there was more, because McFarlane's death further angered the whiskey rebels, and they set fire to John Neville's house.

> Fire had been put to an end of the mansion house, before the fire communicated from the barn and other buildings.

All were consumed; one small building excepted; to which fire was not put, but a guard set over it, at the suggestion of the negroes, that it contained their bacon.

As soon as the house was on fire, the undisciplined of the troops, if I may be allowed the expression; or, as they themselves would say, the unprincipled amongst them, entered, and began to plunder. The cellar was broke [sic] open, and wine and other liquors rolled out, and drank.

"Well, sheee-it! I just know my three-times great-gran-pappy was there. I know he saw the shootin', and I know he saw the sainted martyr McFarlane fall. I see justice in the rebels too. Those rebels didn't burn the slaves' stores. There's got to be more to this John Neville. I see he's the inspector of the whiskey excise, but I'll just bet he's committed even more crimes against mortality."

"Pretty exciting stuff, Hamilton. How about if we leave Mr. Brackenridge's honey hole and do a little prospecting upstream?"

"How's that, Punxie?"

"With your permission, I propose we go back to our search engine and pan for more links."

"Permission granted, brother. I'm all for anything that'll lead us to more about that bastardly bird."

"Roger that," I said. But instead of typing in all manner of Whiskey Rebellion words, I simply typed in "John Neville," and soon after we learned that John Neville had quite a war record and was a big man on the Western Pennsylvania frontier. He fought in the French and Indian War, a conflict that was waged not only to make Canada part of the British Empire, but also to keep all long-standing native inhabitants west of the Allegheny Ridge. Neville also fought in Dunmore's War, a conflict waged to keep all long-standing native inhabitants north of the Ohio and west of the Allegheny Rivers. He was commandant of Fort Dunmore—renamed from the previously abandoned Fort Pitt—and fought in the American Revolutionary War at Trenton, Germantown, Princeton, and Monmouth. As a result, he received many rewards. One was a brevet promotion to Brigadier General given to him by the Continental Congress, an honor without authority or pay. Another was one thousand acres of property.

We already knew Neville owned slaves, but we didn't know that the exact number was sixteen. We also learned that he built the first clapboard house in Western Pennsylvania. While his neighbors lived in log cabins with dirt floors, Neville's house had floors covered with European carpets and plaster walls covered with paper. He filled his library with books and his walls with paintings. He sat in Windsor chairs and slept in a feather bed. And as if that weren't enough, President Washington named General John Inspector of Revenue, which empowered John to collect the whiskey excise tax. Clearly, John Neville had been quite a guy, so much so that the whiskey rebels burned his house to the ground.

Finally, Hamilton and I came upon the matchsticks, or more to the point, an accounting that displayed exactly how Neville and men like him used the excise to enrich themselves and impoverish their neighbors, the very people who, in turn, called the inspector of revenue to account.

Bobbi Lee Versus General John

There it was on the screen in black-and-white. Some historian had done a comparison of the way the 1791 federal excise tax on whiskey—in general, a tax on a specific product at the time of production; more specifically, the first excise tax in American history—advantaged large over small producers. History tells us that the tax was enacted to help our new country pay off its war debt.

The most obvious problem with the scheme was that large distillers paid $.06 per gallon while small distillers paid $.09 per gallon. Of course, every illiterate farmer in Western Pennsylvania knew a bad horse trade when he saw one.

But there was so much more. As Hamilton and I went back and forth between the historical background and the two accounting sheets, we discovered more evils. First off were the disparities between General John and Bobbi Lee's playing fields. On the one hand, General John had the volume and the means to trade in the East Coast cash economy, so he had the money to pay the tax. On the other hand, Bobbi Lee neither had the volume nor the means to trade on the other side of the mountains. Instead, he traded in the Western Pennsylvania barter economy, a place where at best money was scarce. The reality was, Bobbi Lee was cash poor and simply didn't have the money to pay the tax.

The historian also made it clear that men like Inspector of Revenue General John didn't see Bobbi Lee's problem. I said to Hamilton, "Can't you just hear it? 'Of course, you can pay the tax, because after you sell your whiskey, Bobbi Lee, you'll get your money back and then some.'"

"Ain't that just the way, Punxie? The big fish always tryin' to pull the bull over some little fish's eyes."

On top of that, we discovered that small Western Pennsylvania farmers often *paid* a laborer in whiskey and other farm commodities. Why? Because there wasn't money to be had. It was a barter and not a money economy. To add insult to injury, General John had slaves—as did President Washington—so General John had another advantage: unpaid labor.

To make matters even worse, it was likely that Bobbi Lee didn't own his own still. He simply was too poor to pay or barter for this sort of expensive metallic technology. What he probably did instead was pay someone who had the equipment to distill his surplus grain. The distiller's fee was half the output—Bobbi Lee paid the total excise tax as well—so he came away with only *half* the whiskey and paid all the tax on the total amount distilled. Of course, General John had *all* the whiskey to do with what he pleased.

Revelations to be sure. All Hamilton and I could do was drop our jaws and give each other dumbfounded looks, reactions Hamilton punctuated at times with a well-placed, "Sheee-it!"

WHISKEY BOBBI LEE STYLE

grain	- $0.00 *surplus* (9.5 bushels @ $13.1 [$1.38 per bushel])
labor	- $0.00 *diy farmer*
distilling fee	- $21.30 *distiller's fee* (1/2 60 gallons × $0.71)
excise tax	- $5.40 (60 gallon still × $0.09 still under capacity tax to be paid by farmer)
sales	+ $42.60 (60 gallons × $0.71)
profit	<+ $15.90 (*if cash is available*)

WHISKEY GENERAL JOHN STYLE

grain	- $0.00 SURPLUS (95 bushels @ $131 [$1.38 per bushel])
labor	- $0.00 *slave*
distilling	- $0.00 *proprietorially owned*
excise tax	- $36.00 (600 gallon still × $0.06 still filled-to-capacity tax)
sales	+ $426.00 (600 gallons × $0.71 per gallon)
profit	+ $390.00

A Time to Let It Slide

When we were finished learning about Tom the Tinker, John Neville, and the Whiskey Rebellion, Hamilton got really quiet. He sat next to me for a while—I wasn't about to break the silence—and then he got up and walked right out of the Wenatchee Public Library.

I followed Hamilton past Coyote, who was still sitting on the step, trying to divine the truth from that candy wrapper. I followed Hamilton when he turned east toward the Columbia River and then when he turned south, dogging the river's current. I didn't want to chase him, but I also didn't think he was trying to get away.

Finally, I couldn't stand the suspense. I wanted to know what his next move was, so I yelled, "Hey, Hamilton! Where're you going?"

That stopped him, but he didn't turn around, and when I caught up to him, he didn't look me in the eye. Instead, he trained his gaze south, but on what exactly I couldn't tell.

"Like I said, where're you going?"

"Free state," he answered.

"Free state?"

"Me and you, we're goin' to have our own free state."

"Yes, sir. I see the justice in that, but I also see some problems."

"Problems?"

"Yes, sir. It is my belief that free states only stay free if they've got some serious fire power. I don't really see it ending well. You know, helicopters and bullhorns and SWAT teams." I waited for Hamilton to respond, but his only reply was to continue gazing down the Columbia. Then after a minute, maybe two, I picked up where I'd left off. "I've seen enough of bunker busters, Hamilton. Insurgents don't stay insurgents. Insurgents end up as burgers in buns with blood sauce. I've seen on TV what happened at Ruby Ridge and Waco. I know something about Sherman's March to the Sea."

"Bunker busters, huh?"

"Bunker busters, Hamilton."

With that, Hamilton let out a sigh. Oh, he didn't break his gaze south, but he did let out a deep, long sigh, and after that, he said more to the horizon than to me.

"Nah, ain't no threat to *nobody*. Just want to make tax-free whiskey. There's got to be a way."

"I don't know about the tax-free part, Hamilton, but I do like your whiskey business idea. Free enterprise beats slave enterprise any day, and I don't like how the John Nevilles always seem to rig the game against the Bobbi Lees. My dad said he never worked for the big timber companies because he didn't like making money for someone he couldn't look in the eye and have a shot and a beer with."

"Don't like *free state*, huh?"

"Not as much as whiskey business. Personally, I'd like to forget the idea of states altogether. My experience with states is entirely from the bottom. But like I said, the last time almost got me killed."

"Hmm, killed? Nah, don't want none of that."

"But if you want to start up a whiskey business like your three-times great-grandfather whiskey rebel Bobbi Lee, minus the guns and bombs, of course—I want to be clear about that—sure, I could help."

"Whiskey business, huh?"

"Whiskey business."

"Ain't never had a partner, Punxie. But since you said you'd help, I got things to do."

"Like what?"

"Got to scout out materials. Lay a foundation. Put one foot . . . nah, one *bare* foot in front of the other."

"What can *I* do?" I asked.

"Sit tight. I'll be in touch."

"In touch?"

"You'll get a letter."

"How will you know where to send it? I don't have an address." This seemed like a serious snag.

"True, true, an address. Now *there's* somethin' you could do."

"Okay, but when I get an address, how will you know where it is?"

"Got my ways. Faith, brother Punxie. I'll be in touch."

With that, Hamilton started walking again. I could have followed him, maybe I should have, but I suddenly remembered an orderly in the evac hospital, a guy who was cleaning out my bed pan. I couldn't remember his face, but I did remember him telling me that there's a time to sow, and time to reap, a time to get after it, and a time to let it slide. So I let Hamilton walk away.

And that could have been the end of it, but it wasn't, not by a long shot. My first inclination, the one right after I decided not to follow Hamilton, was to go back to the Wenatchee Public Library and sit on the steps next to Coyote. Since I grew up in a library, I knew I'd feel comfortable there, close to my mom. Besides, I also wanted to know what Coyote had to say about that candy wrapper he was reading. I wondered if he could write a review or produce a literary essay. Or maybe what he really had to say would be more like the oracles of Chief Joseph or the prophecies of Isaiah.

Of course, I knew that was silly. After all, the statue was just a hunk of metal—very expressive and evocative to be sure, but a hunk of metal all the same. Instead, I followed my second inclination by turning east and walking until I crossed some railroad tracks and came to the banks of the Columbia River. I stood there for a long time feeling the slow pull of the current. If Coyote and his candy wrapper couldn't help me, then maybe the river's current would have something to say. I mean, that river sure seemed to know where it was going. And even though the Chelan County Public Utility District had its current all damned up, the flow was still traveling, even if it was a crawl, still heading down, down, down to the Pacific. But the longer I stood there, the less my life seemed like a river and more like a series of backwaters: School Slough, the Great Slough of Iraq, Prospectors Slough.

Lost in thought, I watched a leaf slowly float by and then, as if a dam had given way, I felt Pastor Beth and Logger Bob rush in. My muscles felt rigid. It was like a night terror, but I wasn't asleep. I stood very still—me and the Columbia, the Columbia and me—and after the sun slipped below the Cascades, the moon—a clockface that somewhere, somehow had lost its hands—rose above the Columbia Basin.

BETH AND BOB

After learning that my dad and then my mom had died, I didn't know what to think, so I didn't. I wasn't in any shape for that sort news. I mean, I was laid up with a brain pan full of bees in this and that military hospital, and when I was discharged, I didn't go home to Packwood. I didn't return to our sleeping quarters or deal with my parents' possessions. I didn't visit their graves. Instead, I visited bars and taverns in Mossyrock and Morton and a watering hole in Ashford and even another in Onalaska. If I was a lost soul, surely I wasn't the only one.

Avoidance? Sure. I wasn't ready to return to Packwood and have it out with the ghosts of my parents, but apparently, they'd had enough of my pussyfooting around, and now here they were all up inside me in a way they'd never been before: Robert MacLeod Tawney and Elizabeth Margaret Barr-Clay, both still tangled up in the dark romance that made me their only child.

Romance? It started after Beth graduated from the Evergreen State College, Washington State's non-graded liberal arts institution where her parents were professors. After she successfully interviewed with the Timberland Regional Library system, she came to Packwood as its new librarian, and once when I asked her about coming to town, my mom said, "I was thrilled, Punxie. I was in the middle of a dark forest in a building full of books. I felt like I was the princess of Plato's Cave. And then I met your dad."

My dad? He never spoke to me about his childhood, but my mom told me that when my dad was five, his mom, my grandmother, died of cancer. Afterward, my dad said that when he fell asleep, his mom often visited as an angel. Ten years later, his dad, my grandfather, got in a bar fight, was hit in the head outside the tavern, and died shortly thereafter of a brain hemorrhage. And when my dad fell asleep, his dad returned as a demon.

My dad never talked about my mom's arrival to Packwood until I was about to leave for Iraq. As a send-off, he took me to the tavern and—once he'd had a shot and a beer and I'd had one too—looked me in the eye and said, "Boy, she was new in town and the prettiest thing. Right off I peed a ring around her. Beth Barr-Clay was mine. Except, let me tell you, she drove a hard bargain. Only made her prettier, of course. When I told her we were gettin' married, you know what she said? Well, I'll tell you what. She said to me, 'Bob—'" And then he choked up. I'd never seen Logger Bob choked up—there's a first and a last time for everything, I guess—but finally he started up again. "Damn, I can hear her like it's yesterday. See her too. Pretty young thing. Damn . . ." He knocked back the shot and then nodded his head in reverie. "Bartender, pour me another. And another beer too. Same for my boy. Now, where was I? Oh yeh, she said to me, 'Bob, I got my library, and you got your woods, and as long as we keep that straight, I'll stick around.' And I knew it too. She weren't staying for me, and she sure weren't stayin' for Packwood, so it had to be that library. But that was enough."

It was the last time my dad looked me in the eye, and the last time I heard his voice, "Damn straight!" Then he killed the shot, downed the beer, stood, and kicked his chair under the table. As he turned for the door, he said under his breath, "Uh, huh, that was enough."

The Old Wenatchee Bridge

Pop! R-r-r-i-p! Fizz! The memory of my dad walking through the tavern door loosened the pull tab on my beer can of a self and out rushed my parents, spinning, spinning, spinning together until they were gone.

My muscles relaxed.

A dog barked in town, and coyotes yipped up on the ridge across the Columbia.

Some sprinklers started up in a nearby park.

Feeling drained, I wondered about my parents. Had they done what they came to do, said what they needed to say? My mom, the woman who, since birth, had never been in touch with the real world, who strengthened her idealism every day that she went to work, and who would self-destruct if her husband insisted that she be a *real* wife? My dad, the man who, since birth, had been in a grudge match against existence, who strengthened his idealism every time he got fired or quit, and who would self-destruct if his wife insisted that he be a *real* husband? My parents, two singularities, two dark stars pulled into mutual, all-consuming orbit by every fight, every absence, every silence, every sight, sound, touch, taste, and smell.

Add to all that my decision just a few hours earlier to go in with Hamilton on his whiskey project. Back in the library, I thought I had it all figured out. But now I wasn't so sure. Hamilton had come and gone. My parents had come and gone. The leaf I had watched float by was now gone. The whole day—my whole life, in fact—felt untethered.

Standing there by myself, Hamilton seemed less the champion and more the zealot, less my mom and more my dad. Without Hamilton right in front of me, talking to me, exerting his gravitational pull, my future looked less like a rocket to Venus and more like space junk to nowhere. Pretty familiar, really. I'd always been pulled a little this way—by this novel, this game trail—and pulled a little that way—by that drawing, that girl's smile.

Eventually, all the pulling and tugging and wandering made me very tired. I knew I shouldn't just sleep out in the open city, so I started walking with the Columbia's current. Soon, I came to the Old Wenatchee Bridge, and there, under a streetlamp, I found a plaque that told me the bridge was originally built to carry irrigation water. Later, the bridge was modified to include car and truck traffic, but in 1950, when a new bridge was built, this old bridge was closed to motorized vehicles, and now only pedestrians and water passed over.

I checked out the concrete walk ramp that led up to the bridge, but in terms of cover, the ramp was too narrow. The open riverbank on one side of the bridge wasn't inviting, but some closely knit trees on the other side, although not ideal, would at least keep me out of sight.

As I approached, I kept in mind that I wasn't the only drifter looking for shelter. After pushing away some branches, though, I was relieved to find that, at least for now, I was alone. Safe? I had my doubts. But it was enough to convince me to venture in, pick a spot, and clear away a few abandoned items: an empty bottle of malt liquor, a belt buckle in need of a belt, a child's dirty sock. Home sweet home? In America it's called *making do.*

After lying down, I closed my eyes and waited for a pull. I craved a tug. I opened the door to gravitational attraction, but nobody was there. Weightless, I fell asleep.

PART TWO

LETTING IT SLIDE

LETTER TO PUNXIE #1

Hey Punxie

Hitched into town for Sazerac supplies. Looked under the bridge and spotted your backpack and found some shoes and threw them in the river. Like I always say, shoes are the cap screw to the Hindu's hairdo.

Found this notebook and pencil in your backpack. When you get that address, write it down and tuck it between the timbers holdin' up the big pipe goin' up to the bridge.

May the mashbill be untainted

Hamilton

REPLY TO HAMILTON #1

Dear Hamilton,

What the hell? I had to dumpster dive at the thrift store for some shoes. I found some, too, a pair with paint on them the store didn't even want.

And about getting an address: mission accomplished. It all came about because of a gal who reminded me of Marylou in *On the Road* or, better yet, Bonanza Jellybean in *Even Cowgirls Get the Blues*. Picture this—just like in a novel—I was sitting in a diner, and this waitress comes up all snuggly packaged in her pearly buttoned, marigold-colored uniform. I'm telling you, Hamilton, she was one sweet slice of pie—lemon meringue to be exact. She gave me that half wink a girl does when she's offering more than just a short stack of pancakes. I like to think of her as the Aphrodite of Wenatchee, the love goddess of the 4/2 twin coffee maker. When I returned the next day, she kept that high-test coffee of hers coming over the pouty lip of my brown ceramic mug. I imagined her saying, *Another waffle? A piece of apple pie, perhaps? All of our apples are local fruits and picked with loving grace by local virgins. No? Some more coffee then?*

You like that? I figured if I was going to write a letter, I might as well make it interesting. We're all just characters in some crackpot story anyway. Me the down-and-out shell-shocked vet; you the crazy drummer hell-bent on making whiskey. And now, a ripe and juicy, ready-to-pick waitress.

Write back c/o Cherry Kozolowski, The High Voltage Diner, Wenatchee, Washington.

Long Live Free Enterprise,

Punxie

ℓETTER TO ꝓUNXIE #2

Punxie Tawney
c/o of Cherry Kozolowski
The High Voltage Diner
Wenatchee, Washington

Hey Punxie

Characters, huh? Don't know about that, but I do know the foundation's bein' laid.

You see, I spotted the kind of bucket I use for drummin' in a ditch, so I grabbed ahold of that five-gallon bucket, looked up, and saw a sign, Valhalla Substation, the north gods and all, and I knew it was a sign because, like I said, the signs will show you the way.

Thing was, I followed that sign along some electric lines, and at the top of a hill there was a bunch of trans-foreigners, and down off that hill the Rock Island Dam was churnin' out some mighty powerful white water, and right then and there I started drummin' to the electric hum. I'm tellin' you, Punxie, I got good and tranced up, and soon I was groovin' way down deep, and that's when I heard a voice: "You want some fish?"

Like I said, I was all tranced out, so I wasn't sure. I started thinkin' that maybe you're right, Punxie. I'm just a crazy drummer hell-bent on making whiskey. But I'm not shy, so I looked up and here was some guy all decked out in desert camo with an American flag bandana twisted' round his head.

God's truth, Punxie, wasn't sure he was real. Thought he might demysterialize, but he didn't. Instead, he said to me, "I got some big Chinooks in a cooler in my car." And I said back, "Sorry, don't have any money, but the name's Hamilton." He kind of looked me over, really sized me up all the way down to my bare feet, then said, "My name is Ntytyix Kslmix." Wow, I wasn't sure what to do with that, so I said back, "Okay, but slower." He smiled a little and said, "N-tyee-tyee Kslmee." And I said back, "Yep, but can you say that in English?" He smiled a little more and said, "Sure, something like Salmon Sets the Table, but you can just call me Sam the Man." Now that was something I could say, so I said back, "Like salmon, huh? Sam the man, right?" And he shook his head and said, "You catch on quick."

Right after that, I told him about my friend Punxie, and how me and you are goin' to make whiskey like my ancestors way back in Whiskey Rebellion times. And he said that he had this tradin' network all up and down the Columbia and maybe we could do a little business together. I told him that was right up our alley, but did he know a place I could crash? He said he did and took me off the hill to an empty school bus at the back of a junkyard upwind from some migrant shacks. Don't leak. Suits me just fine. It's a place called Malaga right down the river from you.

That's when I asked if I could use his address bein' I needed to get in touch with brother Punxie, and he said that was okay, just write in care of him. I asked if that'd work because I was pretty sure mail comes to an address and not a person. And he said it's okay because everybody knows him here, said *he was* an address around here, and if you put his name, General Delivery, and Malaga on it, it would find him, and later he'd find me.

May the mashbill be untainted

Hamilton

REPLY TO HAMILTON #2

Hamilton Chance
c/o Sam the Man
General Delivery
Malaga, Washington

Dear Hamilton,

That Sam the Man of yours, now he's some character, a real tribal hipster and trader in black market goods. Ntytyix Kslmix? Some native dialect, perhaps, maybe Salish of some sort. But how the hell would a guy like me know? And he says he's got buyers for our product too. I can't wait to meet him.

As for me, drum roll, please . . . I'm packing pears! I put my right hand in. I take my right hand out. I lay the wrapper on, and I tuck it all about. I put it in the carton that will have one hundred count. That's what it's all about! Cute, huh? Besides, I figured I'd lay in some cash while you're putting one *bare* foot in front of the other.

In addition to the money, I got a floor to sleep on. Cherry's got a single room over a vacuum cleaner repair shop, and she lets me in at night and out in the morning. I've got to say she's very cagey. She purrs some, and then her hackles go up. I can't figure out what sets her off. Just when I think she's not going to let me in for the night, she purrs again. And once I'm in, it's the hackles again. Strange, but it beats taking my chances with the urban wildlife of Wenatchee.

In the interest of being let in, I wrote Cherry this little poem. I'm hoping for more purrs, less hackles. It can't hurt, right?

Cherry, my river nymph,
and I her love tramp,
we just opened our eyes
from a big sunrise slap.
Then into the bath
to apply her eyeliner,
and off we both go
to the High Voltage Diner.

The last few mornings I've been slurping coffee and shoveling hotcakes and syrup. Right after that I hoof it down to the Apple Capitol Trail and off to my place of business. They put me on team fruit, and we've been staying ahead of team numbers. No, I don't see this as a steady thing. I don't really think I'm the steady-thing type. I think the fruit and I will get along just fine until the wind blows, a breeze that might just smell a lot like whiskey.

Long Live Free Enterprise,
Punxie

PS: Begging your pardon, sir. You mentioned the word "mashbill" twice. Am I out of line to inquire as to its meaning?

PPS: I put in some stamps and a twenty I found blowing in the wind. How are you eating in that busted-down bus you're in?

ᒪETTER TO ꟼUNXIE #3

Punxie Tawney
c/o of Cherry Kozolowski
The High Voltage Diner
Wenatchee, Washington

Hey Punxie

Mashbill? Sheee-it! That's all what goes into the fermentation. It's all the grains and whatnot. Guess you're a new bee to all this, but you got a nose for what's important, and I like that.

How am I eatin'? Thing is, while I'm waitin' on having a serious powwow with Sam the Man on all things whiskey, I'm killin' time here in Downtown Malaga Centro with this pack of younglins that comes every day and drums with me. They wander in, and we go to wailin', then pretty soon we take a lunch break. It's a beautiful thing because we all share, and then we go back to wailin' until their madres and padres and hermanas and hermanos and tías and tíos and primas and primos come home.

My pack calls me Señor Tambor. We get a groove goin', and sometimes I add in a little somethin' new, but it's mostly about wailin' and keepin' the groove goin'.

For drums, we scrounged up some plastic and metal five-gallon buckets and some old metal sinks. One kid brought a few jerrycans. Sticks're easy enough to find. One kid's partial to rebar.

Yesterday, this madre stopped by to check me out. She said, "Hey, Señor Tambor, you got a regular daycare goin' here. You got government money?" And I said back, "Nah, I don't." And she said, "Hey, Señor Tambor, I don't understand. You got to *live*, you know?" And I said back, "I live just fine. My pack brings their lunches, and we all have one big fiesta: basket tacos, tacos de papa, tacos al pastor, rinds and salsa, queso taquitos. It's a real snoregasboard." When I finished talking, I banged on the bus and said, "I live cheap!" And she said, "Hey, Señor Tambor, you are like the saints in heaven, you know? All the niños y niñas, they love you, you know? All the madres, we love you, you know? I bring you dinner tonight. What you say about that?" And I said back, "Hot damn! Sounds good to me."

And you won't believe what came my way. This same madre came back later and handed me this foil package all made by her and her señoras, and she said, "Hey, Señor Tambor, there's some enchiladas de lengua con salsa verde. You enjoy." And I said back, "Muchas gracias!" And she said, "There is a lot more where that came from. Y muchas gracias a ti también, Santo Tambor."

Sheee-it, Punxie, I've never been called a saint before. You know, the next best thing to makin' whiskey has got to be dreamin' in a junkyard bus all night, wailin' with the niños and niñas all day, and gettin' free delivery from the local madres.

May the mashbill be untainted
Hamilton

REPLY TO HAMILTON #3

Hamilton Chance
c/o Sam the Man
General Delivery
Malaga, Washington

Dear Hamilton,

Saint Chance? Or is it Saint Hamilton? I like Saint Chance. It's got some drama to it, like you're the patron saint of both whiskey makers and card sharks. Yes, sir, it suits you just fine.

I guess you're still waiting to work out the whole whiskey battle plan with Sam the Man. So while you're drumming and eating up a storm, I'll continue with this little subplot I've got going with Cherry.

As you know, I've snagged an address, food, and a job, and yesterday I told Cherry about my time in Iraq and then about my librarian mom and logger dad. Cherry said she couldn't relate to any of that because right after she was born, CPS swooped in—her words—and made her a hot potato in the foster care microwave—my words. I asked her where, and she said she'd been in the Okanagan County CPS system, and next she rattled off towns like Brewster, Twisp, Winthrop, Oroville, Pateros, and Tonasket. "You name it, I lived there," she said. "Oh, not for very long, but I lived there."

I've got to say, Hamilton, it was pretty hard to hear. Her story was all about this little girl who didn't get hit with one IED like me but with a whole bunch, one after another. I mean, I was an adult. I went to the recruiter, and maybe I didn't think it through, but I signed up for what I got. She was just a kid who got drafted and sent to the front lines without a weapon. And when I asked her about the sexual abuse I've heard about, she looked at me really hard. Her eyes were like fingers probing inside me. I don't know if she found what she was looking for, but finally she looked away, and without looking back she touched my hand and asked, "When you were a kid, what'd you do when things got bad?"

I told her I spent a lot of time in the woods exploring, and when the weather turned, I holed up reading in my mom's library.

"Reading, huh? I'm not much of reader," she said and then went on to remember her teachers reading stories out loud while she looked out the window. She said sometimes she'd see Charlotte's web. Other times she'd see the neighborhood go up in flames. At the end, she said, "There was this boy who rode his dirt bike through the field behind the last school I went to. I really wanted to be on the back of that bike. It was right before I aged out."

I told her that I wished I was that boy. I said I would've picked her up and taken her away to someplace better. And she said, "Better? Better like what?"

I had to admit she had me there. Truthfully, I said I didn't know, but that I thought anything had to be better than foster care or Iraq. After that, I asked her if she wanted to go for a walk. I figured we could use a change of scenery.

We ended up taking a stroll west of the Old Wenatchee Bridge, and eventually we came upon a derelict brick fire station, one that had been built like a medieval castle with battlements and an octagonal turret off on the left side. The turret had four second-story windows that made me think of eyes. One stared to the south, one to the southeast, one to the northeast, and one—the sleepy one with a half-pulled shade—out to the river. I liked that eye the best. The other two windows on the second story were above an arched set of double garage doors. The windows had been bricked over and the garage doors shut tight against time.

But for all the neglect, there were also signs of life. For one, there was a banner stretched across the garage doors.

CATACOMBS USED BOOKS

For another, there was a door below the shaded eye-like window, and once I saw that the door was open, my reading jones came on *hard*.

Why? Because when I got shipped overseas to Iraq, I quit reading. I was on the wagon. I went cold turkey. True, my mom sent a few books in a care package, but I couldn't read them. Why again? Because war zones aren't libraries. Too many people. Too close quarters. Too much noise. Too much unpredictability. Some doctor in the evac hospital called it the dopamine switch. He said dopamine puts you on the edge of your seat waiting, waiting, waiting. But the problem with war, or any trauma for that matter, is that a soldier's switch gets stuck and won't turn off. He said, "Think of it like gravity at Niagara Falls; the dopamine just keeps pulling everything over the edge."

He was right too. There I was in Anbar Province, waiting for the next order, the next siren, the next rocket round, and *boom!* Like a card trick gone wrong, my brain got thrown to the desert winds. *Boom!* My dad got impaled by a falling tree limb, a *real* window-maker, or so my mom's letter said. *Boom!* My mom took a handful of sleeping pills and chased it with a bottle of vodka, or so my mom's suicide note said, the one the police forwarded my way. And finally, the American military *boomed* my shell-shocked ass back into the American wilds.

But when I saw that open door, I felt the old childhood craving—the one my mom turned me on to and fed in her library—slowly seep back in. Print. Plot. Characters. Setting. Style. Theme. Narrative, the whole nine yards and more. Wild imagination. Elegant order. The joy of nonsense. The comfort of sense. And like a junkie with a dime bag just out of reach, I wanted . . . no, I needed a hit.

"Let's go inside," I blurted out.

"I told you I'm not much of a reader," Cherry barked back.

"I know, but used bookstores are like libraries. You never know what you'll find. It'll be an adventure. What do you say?"

"Whatever you say, *boss*." She stabbed the word *boss* like it was a sarcasm accelerator on a Fast Attack Vehicle. Her snipe was so sharp that it startled, even scared me. I didn't understand how my simple request triggered such a response.

But clearly Cherry's shock didn't equal the bookstore's allure because I immediately forgot she was there, and like the reading freak that I was and still am, I headed for the promised land. A place to relax. A place to heal. A place to escape. And once inside, I heard a woman's voice. I couldn't see the woman, but her voice had a French accent and came from somewhere in an aisle between all the shelves piled high with books.

"*Bonjour, mes amis.*"

"Oh, hi," I said.

"*Bienvenue.*"

"Uh huh," Cherry said. Apparently, she had followed me in. As preoccupied as I was, I hadn't noticed.

"*N'hésitez pas.* Feel free."

"Thanks," I responded. Still self-absorbed, I began to wander and explore—checking out *Zen and the Art of Motorcycle Maintenance* and then picking up *The Electric Kool-Aid Acid Test*—until I came to a box canyon blocked by an Abyssinian cat perched on a stack of *Oz* magazines. I thought about giving that cat a pet, but then I wasn't sure—it's hard to say with cats. Instead, I turned around, and there was Cherry. She was standing behind me, and clearly she wasn't happy.

"Want to head out? I asked.

"Uh huh," Cherry said under her breath and began to make her way toward the entrance.

Although I fell in line behind her, it wasn't easy to leave. Truthfully, I wanted to ask the French voice if I could rent an aisle and move in, but I figured I'd stick with the temperamental cat that I knew, the one with a room of her own, the one who sometimes purred.

As we neared the door, we came across the woman whose voice had greeted us. She was like a small, round owl wrapped in a pale green sweater covered in lint bunnies. A pair of leopard-spot, cat-eye glasses dangled from a chain around her neck, and her smile was painted with bruise-purple lipstick.

"*Regarde, ces livres sont pour toi.*"

"Excuse me?" I said.

"These books." She smiled, pointing to three paperbacks and then to Cherry. "They are for you, no?"

"Those?" Cherry asked doubtfully.

"*Qui.*"

The books in question rested atop a bookcase stuffed with novels. From what I could gather, the books were all written by women and all translated from French into English.

"Twenty dollars, no?"

"I don't know these books," I said.

"*Et toi, mon cheri*?"

"I don't read much," Cherry answered.

"O-o-o-o-h, but you do, *dans tes rêves*, no?"

"What," Cherry said. It wasn't a question.

"In your dreams. You read there, no?"

"Maybe," Cherry said. Her tone wasn't hopeful.

"*Alors*, allow me to me choose. *Première, The Juggler*, no?"

"Okay," I answered.

"*Deuxième, The Pure and the Impure*, no?"

"Sure," I answered again. Cherry clearly wanted no part in this transaction.

Then the proprietress laughed. "And *dernière, Les Guérrillères, qui, qui*." She laughed again. "The first two are for you, mademoiselle. This one is for the monsieur." She laughed once more.

"I don't know," Cherry said. It was hard for her to be polite.

"Oh, but I do," the proprietress said, turning to me. Her delightful smile turned a bit conspiratorial. "You read to her. Then she read to you. Then you read to her, one page at a time, *et ainsi de suite*, no?"

"I think we can do that," I said and handed the old but lively French lady a twenty. She folded and stuffed the bill down her bra. After I took the books, Cherry and I walked out the door and into a shadowless afternoon.

Good story, right, Hamilton? Interesting characters and setting. Every word, and I swear this to be true, is exactly as I experienced it. Real *verité*, a word I picked up reading movie reviews.

But enough about me. How's the saint gig going? Blessed any communion tacos?

Long Live Free Enterprise,

Punxie

ℓetter to Punxie #4

Punxie Tawney

c/o of Cherry Kozolowski

The High Voltage Diner

Wenatchee, Washington

Hey Punxie

Good news. Sam the Man visited, and we had a sit-down around the burn barrel and shared some of my Sazerac and some of his smoked salmon, and then we shared some more Sazerac and smoked salmon, and after about the fifth share, I told him more about making tax-free whiskey and about my granpappy and everything he told me about Westsylvania. He said Westsylvania was four counties in Pennsylvania. Mingo Creek was in one, you can be sure of that. He also said there were two more counties in Virginia, and all the counties called themselves Westsylvania because they didn't see eye to eye with the new U S of A. They were all up in the Whiskey Rebellion. And after that I told him that me and brother

Punxie was goin' to bring back Westsylvania somewhere around here. So what did he think of that?

And you know what, Punxie? Sam the Man told me exactly what he thought. He said to me, "Beats the Drum"—that's what he's callin' me now—"I got some idea about where that might be." And I said, "Nah, what you mean?" And he said, "I got a place where you can make tax-free whiskey, and if you go there, I can sell that whiskey. No problem. It's less than an hour away from right where we're sitting."

Sheee-it! I'm tellin' you, Punxie, you'd better get yourself off that Cherry. Get your head straight, brother. Get yourself back on some good, clean, made-in-America whiskey. Better yet, on some tax-free, made-in-Westsylvania whiskey!

May the mashbill be untainted
Hamilton

REPLY TO HAMILTON #4

Hamilton Chance
c/o Sam the Man
General Delivery
Malaga, Washington

Dear Hamilton,

I see you've heard back from Sam the Man about a possible base camp. I understand that this new site, should it be feasible, is to be called Westsylvania. Thank you for providing me with the historical details surrounding the naming of our potential new base, a most appropriate choice to be sure. This is exciting news, sir, and I await further instructions. It should be fun and possibly profitable. It'll make for a good story too.

Speaking of stories, here's what's happening with Cherry. It wasn't easy, but Cherry and I started reading *The Juggler.* I started us out, and when it was Cherry's turn, she said I was doing so good I should keep going. Of course, I told her that's not what the French lady said, but Cherry said, "Fuck the French lady. Just keep reading." So I did.

Not too far in, I figured out that *The Juggler* is one sexy book. No, it's not the pornography we know and love, none of that slam-bam-that's-my-jam kind of thing. It all starts out with this juggler woman, and she's too cool to be in love with a man because, get this, she's in love with a vase. In addition, she's got all these ivory and wax figures straight out of *The Kamma Sutra,* and she brews up this wild coffee drink with funked-up spices. And there's more! Her place smells of incense and essential oils, a real hippie chick's pad. And if I'm being perfectly honest, the whole thing makes me cum just thinking about it.

But I stopped reading when the juggler woman said, "Women don't write, they sign!" She said it like it was some big philosophical pronouncement, and I told Cherry I didn't get it because everybody knows any woman with a pencil can write.

It seems like a reasonable observation, right? Apparently not, because Cherry came right back at me. I mean, she stood straight up over me, looked really angry, and said, "You *want* to get it?"

I didn't know what to say. I didn't understand how the whole thing had suddenly gone from sexy to weird. I felt like I was in Iraq, the insurgents were out there, and I was under fire. I really did. I didn't know how to respond, but without thinking, the word *sure* came out of my mouth.

Cherry shot back, "Okay, asshole, feel and learn." And then she told me to take off my pants. It's not like she hadn't seen me with my pants off, so I did what she said. The situation was moving too fast for me to do much else.

Next, she used my belt to bind my feet together and told me to take off my shirt. Again, I did what she said. It was like I was some actor in a porno.

After she used her belt to bind my hands behind my back, she went outside, knocked on the door, and said she was the police. What was I going to do? I couldn't get up and answer the door, so I told her to come in, and no sooner did she open the door, she said to me, "I got this court order signed by a judge pursuant to the penal code that says you got to make me happy."

"What?" I asked.

"If you don't make me happy, you're out on the street. And if you still don't make me happy, it's the mental institution for you, boy. You're in for some serious electroshock. That ought to fix you right up, keep you from getting all emotional, you useless bitch."

"What the hell?" It was all I could come up with.

"You don't get it, do you?"

"No, not really."

"Well, let me tell you. All men are stupid fucks, but since I like your kind of stupid fuck, let me ask you something. Why do you think I stripped you and tied you up?"

"I was wondering about that."

"I tied you up because now you're me. See, I wrote, cast, and directed you as the woman."

"O-o-o-kay."

"And then I wrote, cast, and directed myself as the police-*man* who orders little helpless you to do things you can't possibly do because you're all tied up. And why are you tied up?"

"Uh, because you tied me up?"

"Bingo! But you didn't know that I'd already written, cast, and directed myself as the police*man*."

"I guess not."

"And under what power did I order you to make me happy or face the consequences of homelessness where you can only make me happy by being my whore or put in a nuthouse where your brain will be fried like a plantain?"

"A judge?"

And where does the judge's power come from?"

"Some law?"

"Double bingo! Men write laws that give them power. Men write scripts where women are powerless. It's all a power trip, the battle of the sexes and all that shit, except women don't have any weapons or courts or even a goddamn, motherfucking pencil! All women can do is tie up our boyfriends to teach them a lesson. Men write. Women sign."

"I don't know what to say, Cherry."

"Got nothing to say, huh? Did I steal your pencil? Cat scratch your tongue out?"

"Maybe."

"Well, maybe this stupid fuck's got it!"

Maybe I did, and maybe I didn't. But after all that, I got to say, and this may seem a bit weird, I do see my parents differently. My dad used to complain about my mom's backbone. He said it was made out of carbon tool steel. He used to scream and yell at her about not doing what he said, and she'd just stand there, not say a word, and he'd slam the door and go to the tavern. The next morning she'd make breakfast and then head off to the library as if nothing had happened. Battle of the sexes? It's not Iraq, but I guess it's a battle all the same.

And as for Cherry, she didn't kick me out, but she didn't purr either.

Long Live Westsylvania,

Punxie

Letter to Punxie #5

Hey Punxie,

Cain't say I really understand what's goin' on, but I'm not interested in what you're fightin'. Pretty much steered clear of that sort of thing. You dropped a bad cherry in your mash, and now you got to throw out the whole batch. Just forget about it. Time to groove on what me and Sam the Man are layin' down.

You see, Sam the Man stopped by, and he said to me, "Hey, Beats the Drum, it's time to go to Westsylvania." And I said back, "Not possible, Sam the Man. Thing is, Westsylvania's no place on this earth. I talk like it's a real place, but I'm on to myself. Like my granpappy used to say, 'That boy Hamilton, he's full of sheee-it. It's just the way he talks.' " But Sam the Man wasn't havin' none of that because he said, "Really, Beats the Drum? I've been there. It's on Whiskey Dick Creek." And I said back, "Whiskey Dick Creek?" And he said, "Yes, Whiskey Dick Creek." And I said back, "Huh, I like the sound of that. Maybe it's a sign. Maybe it's one of those fishins of immorality."

I'm tellin' you, Punxie, Westsylvania was callin', so me and Sam the Man piled into his Woody Wagon and headed up your way and crossed over the river and headed south down to Palisades Road and straight into someplace called Moses Coulee. Never seen anything like it, just a canyon all walled in with basalt cliffs. We then started up that canyon a ways until we come to this farmhouse, and Sam the Man made a hard left onto this dirt track and then another hard left. "Old railroad grade, Beats the Drum," he said. And then he made a hard right through a sorry excuse for a creek. "Douglas Creek, Beats the Drum." And then a hard right into a hairpin. "Hold onto your hat, Beats the Drum." And then into another hairpin, only this one's wider, and then we made a hard stop. "Now we walk, Beats the Drum."

After we piled out, we started walkin' maybe two hundred fifty yards on the hard pack until we come to this break in the basalt cliff that led up out of Moses Coulee. "Whiskey Dick Creek, Beats the Drum!" he declared. And I said back, "You got to be kiddin' me, Sam the Man." And he said, "You want to find your Westsylvania?" And I said back, "You know I do!" And he said, "This is the easiest way."

You know, brother Punxie, I didn't know what I was gettin' myself into. Thing was, we were fixin' to step on through a chink in this ravine. Maybe my bare soles weren't up to the challenge. But like I always say, nothin' measured, nothin' chained, so we started walkin' on the dead basalt followin' that goddamned stain called Whiskey Dick Creek. It was tough goin'. Wasn't so much of a path as a line where the lichens had been worn off the rocks.

There was a sickly lookin' tree and a little bit farther up a patch of scrub and then a fork. "This way, Beats the Drum." I would've gone left, but Sam the Man, he went right, and we crawled up the draw some more until Sam the Man hopped across Whiskey Dick Creek. There's no water, but he jumped anyway, and I followed. A real hell in a hambasket, I say.

And right then Sam the Man pointed at a cliff. "Up there, Beats the Drum. That's Westsylvania." And I said back, "Huh?" And he said, "Up there. Westsylvania's up there." And I said back, "You got to be kiddin' me?" And he said, "I don't kid." And you know, Punxie, this Sam the Man's really somethin' else.

For one, he knows his way around here like a momma knows her baby's butt. And let me tell you, he's got the eagle eye, and that's for sure.

For another, he knows everybody on every reservation and in every orchard. He told me about all the reservations and all the tribes and so many kinds of names that I just don't know, but he knows them all. And he said he picked fruit when he was a kid with all kinds of people from all the tribes and all the Mexican states. But he doesn't do that anymore because he's got his own thing goin'. I got to say, Punxie, I'm not exactly sure what Sam the Man's thing is, but it's like if you cooked up an Indian chief with some gang leader and a bit of Robin Hood and put it all in one big voodoo pot, well . . . yep! I'd say Sam the Man's that kind of gumbo.

And sometimes he's funny. This one time he was talkin' about Coyote, and it made me think of that statue we saw in front of the library. He said to me, "Hey, Beats the Drum, Coyote and me, we were out for a drive along the Columbia, and Coyote says, 'I'm thirsty. I could drink all that damn water, you know.' So Coyote and me went out to Crescent Bar, which is just this big desert flood plain off the Columbia, and we drove out on West Bar Road. And you know what old Coyote said to me? He said, 'Damn, what good are all these dams if all these bars are dry?' "

Funny, huh? But gettin' back to Westsylvania. Sam the Man said to me, "Climb, Beats the Drum." And I said back, "But . . ." And he said, "Trust me, Beats the Drum. It's not hard. Look, there are places to grab onto and places to put your feet. Scientists say those places were made by gas bubbles long ago, but I say two women had a big argument and their angry words left these holes." I said back, "If you say so." And he said, "Okay, up we go, Beats the Drum."

Now, I wasn't goin' first, so I watched Sam the Man use the holes like a ladder, and soon I was followin' behind, and in no time we were standin' on this ledge. It was about twenty feet deep or so and ended at a cave, and above that cave the cliff shot up some more.

I got to say, Punxie, I didn't think much of the place at first. It looked like everything else. But while I was thinkin' all that, Sam the Man said, "But you know, Beats the Drum, you need to call this place something different." And I said back, "I do? What's that?" And he said, "You need to call this place Westcoulatum. You know, West Cool A Tum. Cool, like in Coulee." And I said back, "My granpappy told me *penn* is for *William Penn*, and *sylvan* is just another way to say *trees*. Nothin' sylvan about this place. Not a Penn or a tree in sight. Maybe you got somethin' there." And he said, "You know I do, Beats the Drum." And I said back, "Give me some time. I got to think on that some, Sam the Man. Yep, give me some time." And he said, "You do that, Beats the Drum. You take some time. But you know I'm right."

The thing is, Punxie, the more I think about it, the more Westcoulatum's beginnin' to grow on me. The way I see it, Westcoulatum's got a future. You need to dump out that mash with the bad cherry and get your ass down here. We're goin' to have one big tax-free, whiskey makin', all-you-can-live freedom buffet!

May the mashbill be untainted

Hamilton

PART THREE

DISTILLING FREEDOM

Choice

After I read Cherry Hamilton's last letter, she leveled both barrels, drew a bead, and fired. "I'm not standing between you and your *boyfriend*. You're not hanging that one on *me!*"

Wow, boyfriend? I wanted to tell her to stop with the crazy talk, but I didn't because if I'd learned one thing about Cherry, it was that she was an in-your-face gal. And if I was being honest, she had a point. It was true, I'd raised my flag in two camps, and clearly that wasn't going to fly because neither Cherry nor Hamilton recognized dual citizenship. Hamilton had said as much, and now Cherry, with hands on hips, was saying the same.

My problem was that I've had very little practice choosing. In my experience, life had always been done to me. I really hadn't done much to life. True, I went to college, and I joined the Army, but at the time neither felt like choices. I've always preferred to think of my life as a road without junctions or forks. Back then, college and the Army were just stops that didn't go my way.

But at the moment, none of that mattered because Cherry— the abused foster child, now battle-scarred woman—didn't give a damn about what I preferred. She was muscling me while the words in my head raced like a fast mountain stream; while the words in my ears rambled on about being a rotten apple, like I wasn't good for sauce, or even juice; while the words in my mouth came tumbling out, words about getting settled, about getting the lay of Hamilton's land, and about Cherry paying a visit . . . maybe. I mean, everyone deserved a little freedom, didn't she think?

And right after I said the word *freedom*, Cherry'd had enough. "Freedom, Punxie? Well, fuck you. You're going to lay that freedom shit on me? I know where this is going. Freedom this. Freedom that. Every time someone says freedom, that means freedom from me. But don't you worry about me. I'm used to being told, 'Fuck you.' I'm used to being locked out. I'm used to the door slamming and never seeing some shithead again. You're no different. You're just another piece of shit, and I can flush you like all the rest."

And then she stopped, a bit of a lull in the storm, but I knew there was more. Right after the pause she shuddered, said, "Goddamn you," and let drop an actual tear—a scalding tear, a molten tear, a radioactive tear, but the only tear—followed by a fierce squall: "I invited you here. I fed you. I made room in my bed for you. I let you put your hands all over me. I let you *inside me*. And now you want to pull that freedom shit on me? Well fuck you, Punxie. *Your* kind of freedom is *my* eviction notice."

Bang. There it was again, that shell-shocked feeling, and the only response I could muster was, "Sorry."

"Sorry?" And I don't know how she pushed a crooked smile through all that rage. It was eerie. It really was. "*Sorry?* You know, Punxie, maybe, just maybe, I'll take you up on it. Maybe I'll just crash your little freedom party since *you* offered and all. Uh huh, maybe I will."

Then she came over and kissed me harder on the mouth than was necessary. Her tongue was cold-blooded, like a six-inch cut-throat trout, and when she was done, she spun on one heel—no way I was making her late for her evening shift at the High Voltage Cafe—and blew out the door.

CHIEF MOSES

After Cherry left for work, I walked down to the Columbia River, and when I got there, the river looked sad. When I thought about that sadness, it seemed the river was thinking way too much about the past, remembering the crazy mad rush, reliving the one-night stands around every bend all the way to the Pacific. I knew that it wasn't a young-man river anymore. It was an old-man river, and a damned-up one at that.

And out of this sadness I remembered a story that a guy once told me. I had stopped along these very banks, only I was a mile upstream, maybe more like a mile and a half, and I was coming home from work. I was tired from a long day of packing pears. I had started the morning packing Anjou pears, and then the foreman came by and told me to go to a different line and pack Bosc pears. After that, I left my place of work. I was tired from packing pears and came down to the Columbia River.

The story was about Chief Moses, the once-great chief of the Sinkiuse-Columbia and the man for whom Moses Coulee was named, the place where Hamilton had gone to make whiskey. He was known to be a very powerful man and often rode his horse down through Moses Coulee and crossed the Columbia near where I was standing. Of course, back then, Moses didn't call the river Columbia. Moses didn't even call himself Moses; that was something the Presbyterian Missionary Henry Spaulding did.

When Chief Moses and his horse swam across the Columbia, they would start by walking into the river; then they would begin to swim because the current would take away their feet. While they swam, Moses always had a hold of his horse's mane, and he always stayed upstream from his horse. He never was downstream from his horse. He didn't want to tire his horse by becoming a weight dragging his horse downstream.

Chief Moses only crossed the river this way when there were important people on the other side. He was also known for always coming late to a party. He wanted to make a grand entrance and surely was quite a sight. After all, there must have been a reason why Henry Spaulding and all the other White folks called him Moses.

When I was done remembering the story, I wondered if people who swam in the river were washed of their memories. When I was off the job and Cherry was busy with hers, I'd read up on Chief Moses in the Wenatchee Public Library. I wondered if Chief Moses was washed of the Blackfeet warrior that he killed when he was fifteen, or of his trip to Washington, DC, where he got sick on foie gras, or even of the day he spent digging roots when the sun sat on the mountains and never went down. And what if all these memories, the ones of Chief Moses and everyone else, were piling one upon the other, what with the Rock Island and Wanapum and Priest Rapids and McNary and John Day and The Dalles and Bonneville Dams?

Then I imagined walking into the river and letting its sad, slow current take away my feet. It felt fitting for the river to be sad and for me to be sad and then for both of us to join hands. I thought our merging might give us a sort of beauty. At least, that's what I thought.

But I was too much of a coward to give myself up to history, and I also realized I was too much of a coward to turn around and walk into the future with Cherry. She said I was a piece of shit, and I had no evidence to the contrary. Clearly, she had been following Hamilton's and my letters and waiting for what she thought was inevitable: the scene where a man tells a woman one thing and then does another.

Argue? I'd never been one to do that, so like I've always done, I continued into the future, on to that single road without junctions or forks, across the Old Wenatchee Bridge, and then south toward Moses Coulee and all that would come next.

The Moses Coulee ICU

"Where y'headed, young fella?"

"South a bit."

"Me too. Hop in." And after I did, the driver said, "Am I droppin' y'off local, or are y'headin' to parts unknown?"

"Local. Moses Coulee to be exact. You know about Moses Coulee?"

"Know it? I *am* Moses Coulee. Ninety years old if I'm a day. I's born below Three Devils. I lived my whole life below Three Devils. And I'm goin' to be buried below Three Devils. What y'think 'bout that, young fella?"

"That's something."

As I settled into the leather upholstered bench seat, I took a liking to the old-timer's car. The ride felt smooth, but after I fully appreciated the padded dashboard and aviation-style instrumentation, I thought a compliment might grease the wheels.

"Nice car."

"Yeh, we've been together since fifty-two."

"I know a little bit about old cars. The people where I come from never have new cars, just old ones, but I don't know about this one."

"This one here's a Kaiser Virginian. I bought it in Wenatchee when I's 'bout thirty. I came into town, sold twenty head, and paid cash. I thought I was somethin' back then. Still do, if y'want to know the truth."

"I didn't know Kaiser made cars."

"I expect there's a lot you don't know, young fella. And I can't say that I recognize you. Nobody, and I mean *nobody*, comes to Moses Coulee, at least since they shut down the railroad."

"I'm visiting a friend."

"Good friend or bad friend?"

"I'm not sure what you mean."

"Well, when you get to be my age, and good luck if y'do, you'll learn all 'bout bad friends. But that's a thing I can't tell y'bout. No, that's somethin' different."

"I guess I'm going to find out."

"Good answer. Better than most."

We drove past orchards: some pear, mostly apple, a few cherry. The trees, the ones that stretched between the Columbia River and the highway, were all carefully manicured, and as I looked out the window, the trees made me think of child stars. I began to wonder what would happen when they grew up. Would they be addicted to nitrates? Would they become covered with canker? Would they die lonely in some dive motel off the main road on the other side of town?

And before long, the Kaiser Virginian slowed to a stop at an intersection; then the old-timer smoothly turned us left into what I presumed was Moses Coulee. To my left, the basalt wall of the Columbia Gorge steeply dropped down to the coulee floor. Then to my right, the basalt wall abruptly rose again. I imagined a sign stretching across the entrance to Moses Coulee: "PEARLY GATES." No, not a chance. "ABANDON ALL HOPE." Again, I didn't think so. This place didn't care that much.

DON'T GIVE A FUCK

Now that seemed about right.

As we headed in, the coulee floor became an expanse of desert hemmed in on either side by basalt walls. I didn't feel like I was riding on planet Earth, but when I thought about it some more, I supposed all this was the original stuff, and when I thought about it even more, this basalt desert had dibs on all the chainsawed clearcuts I grew up with.

A bit farther in, we came out of the basalt fields and drove through some more fruit trees. I knew this was an orchard because I could see the plumes of irrigation water. Orchards on the moon? Desolation apples? The orchard also brought to mind a painting that hung over the circulation desk in my mom's Packwood Library. My mom said it was called *American Progress*, but I remembered it as *American Angel* because I spent my pubescent years imagining what was beneath the giant woman's flimsy nightgown, the one she wore while flying above the landscape. Back then, I'd gaze up at her day after rainy day, convinced that she didn't have on underwear. But now when I bring that painting to mind, I see Madame Progress flying out from the rising sun. Behind her to the east are the Brooklyn Bridge and westbound trains. Running with her are westbound stagecoaches and farmers. Running away to the west are bears, Indians, and buffalo. I also remember that Madame Progress carries a schoolbook in her right hand and is laying telegraph line with her left. And although she once brought me visions of getting laid, it's clear to me now that this painting was missing one thing: a Columbia Plateau orchard with its irrigation plumes.

But after the old-timer and I drove out of the orchard, we came upon more basalt cliffs, and that's when, and I swear this to be true, I heard the lichens snicker, the same chuckle I heard when I sized up the highlands of Iraq's Anbar Province. No, it wasn't a full belly laugh because, really, what's the point? Lichens like these have been on Iraqi limestone and Moses Coulee basalt forever, which, if you ask me, just makes the orchard, the one I'd just passed through, look plain silly, what with its irrigation IV lines and fertilizer feeding tubes. It seems to me this orchard should have been named the Moses Coulee

ICU. I'm telling you, those trees were living on borrowed time, expensive time at that.

END OF THE LINE

"So, where you meetin' your friend, young fella?"

"He tells me there's this farmhouse on the right, but you turn left before you get to the farmhouse. He says he's up Whiskey Dick Creek."

"Whiskey Dick, huh?"

"Yes, sir. That's what he said. He's up Whiskey Dick Creek. Do you know it?"

"Do I know it? Do I *know* it? Let me tell you somethin', young fella. I told you I know *everythin'* about Moses Coulee. And let me tell you somethin' else. There isn't a single thing *to* know. I think your friend's either cracked in the head or thinks you're cracked in the head. So, you cracked in the head, young fella?"

"I suppose I am."

"That's good. Uh huh, and you know what young fella, I *suppose* I am too. I've lived at the dead end of Moses Coulee my whole life, and did I tell you I'm ninety years old? Yeh, I probably got the dry rot. No, I surely got the dry rot." And the old-timer turned and opened up a smile that for all the world looked like a cemetery, except the tombstones in his mouth were all made of gold, and the sun came through the windshield in such a way that his smile was blinding.

"As I's sayin', up here's a sort of road. I say it's a sort of road because it don't go nowhere. All the roads off this one go but nowhere. But it does stop after a fashion at Whiskey Dick Creek. Mind you, Whiskey Dick is only a sort of creek."

Once again, the Kaiser Virginian slowed. We hadn't seen a single car the whole time we were in Moses Coulee, and then the old-timer eased us into a left turn, the one Hamilton had told me about in his last letter. We drove slowly this way on a dirt track and back that way on a dirt track, and then we were driving not at all.

"End of the line, young fella."

"Much obliged. How much farther is it to Three Devils?"

"Oh, a ways. Could be less. Could be more."

"Well, like I said, much obliged."

I opened the door, grabbed my backpack, and as I went to close the door, I heard the old-timer say, "Cracked in the head? Suppose I am. Yeh, that's a good one."

The Whiskey Dick Cathedral

I started walking. I had the southern sun at my back so that the approaching ravine shimmered like one of Monet's paintings. I wondered what old Claude Monet would have done if he'd have set up shop right here on top of this basalt.

Monet, right? Sure, I grew up in the woods and got my butt blown clear out of Iraq, but like I've said, I had a mom who handed me *The Adventures of Huckleberry Finn* and *Of Mice and Men* and *The Catcher in the Rye*, not to mention *Don Quixote* and later *Slaughterhouse-Five*, and a dad who threw people my way—all folks I learned to appreciate as characters.

I've also said that I spent many childhood days soaking up art books while Pacific rains fell endlessly about. One of my favorite art books had a series of Monet's world-famous, time-lapse paintings of the Rouen Cathedral. Even as a child, I found Monet's art fascinating, especially his idea that objects change their appearance as the sun tracks across the sky. Now an adult, I stopped and imagined Claude Monet painting thirty canvases of the entrance to Whiskey Dick Creek.

But it didn't end there because right after imagining Monet painting, I saw what came next: the Moses Coulee gift shops selling pieces of *real Moses Coulee basalt* along with the Moses Coulee tour buses filled with picture-snapping tourists, all balding, all in Hawaiian shirts and Bermuda shorts, all toting Colossal Huge Swigs, all, just like me, squinting to see what Claude Monet saw when he came to Moses Coulee.

And then I heard the song that I learned over in Iraq, the tune soldiers parodied from Country Joe and the Fish, the one that went, "And it's one, two, three, what are we fighting for? Don't ask me, I don't give a damn, next stop's Afghanistan!"

TICKET TO FREEDOM

To get that song out of my head, I started walking, and as I entered the ravine, the song quit playing. Instead, my brain played something different, a thought that said the moon had nothing on Moses Coulee. Then that thought became another, that Moses Coulee had nothing on Whiskey Dick Creek. And as I continued walking, the ravine proved to be soul-sucking and ankle-busting. Each step came down in the only place available and often landed at an opposing angle to the last. It didn't take long for another thought to come to mind, something about walking through the valley of death.

But just as I was about to turn around and hitchhike my way back to Cherry, I heard Hamilton yell, "Sheee-it! Is that Punxie Tawney walkin' right past his ticket to freedom! Come on, brother! Haul your ace up here."

Ah, a friendly voice, one coming from a rock ledge that was down a side ravine and halfway up a cliff face. After I closed the distance, all I could see was basalt. Sure, I could see the hollows in the cliff face that Hamilton had written about, but I had my doubts, so I called up, "Now what?"

"See the holes in the rock?"

"Yes, sir."

"Easier than it looks. Sam the Man said so, and he's right. Like I said in my letter, just like a ladder. Climb on up."

I'll be the first to admit that I'm no mountain climber, so I started out slowly. But after taking advantage of a toehold and then a handhold and then another toehold, I got the hang of it. I've got to say my experience with that basalt was up close and personal. So close, in fact, that I noticed this particular basalt wasn't just slate gray, not by a long shot. Sure, there was some of that, but there were also blues and whites and browns and yellows and oranges and greens, and even a bit of sparkle. It was subtle, but visually speaking, this was some very complex geology.

And right then I saw Hamilton's hand dangling directly over my head.

ℋAMILTON'S 𝒲ESTCOULATUM

Hamilton's Westcoulatum rested on a basalt ledge halfway up a basalt cliff. The sky above was blue. I liked to think it was a woman's sheer-blue negligee worn to make everything below much more appealing. But what really stood out was the make-shift building that looked to me like a Confederate general's artillery battery and a Neanderthal's mining entrance and the devil's depot all rolled into one.

No, I'm not using metaphors just to be poetic. I'm being accurate, which is to say that Hamilton's Westcoulatum really had to be seen to be believed, and it all came about when some-one—maybe Sam the Man, I certainly didn't know—partially assembled a square building from discarded eight-and-a-half-foot railroad ties, maybe ones that had become useless when the trains quit coming to Moses Coulee.

The first wall of railroad ties came straight out from the upper cliff face, the thirty feet of basalt that acted as the termi-nus for the back of the ledge.

The second wall of railroad ties came at a right angle off the first wall and ran parallel to both the upper cliff face and the ledge's edge.

The third wall, the one that should have connected the sec-ond wall back to the cliff face, was no wall at all. It was open air.

And the fourth wall, well, it was just the upper cliff face, but it was open air, too, because the wall of basalt was under-mined by a five-foot-tall, ten-foot-deep cave, a feature that turned out to be valuable because inside the cave, Hamilton had found a seep. Here, he collected water in a one-by-four galvanized stock tank—*drip, drip, drip, drip, drip*—the West-coulatum Water Works.

"What you think, Punxie?" Hamilton said now that I was standing on the ledge next to him.

"I don't know what to say."

"Takes your breath away, don't it? Freedom's like that. I always say freedom's a butt punch that knocks the shit right out of a man."

Good Squatters

The tour of Hamilton's Westcoulatum started with the railroad tie building. I asked Hamilton who dragged the railroad ties up here and for what purpose. He said he asked Sam the Man the same question, and Sam the Man told him he didn't know, that maybe they were a temple Coyote built to the two ladies who had the big argument, the squabble that made the hand-and-toeholds we used to climb up to the ledge.

Then Hamilton told me to throw my backpack in a corner of the structure, and I stood for a minute and tried to take it all in. Again, my brain only settled on metaphors for this place, something like a derelict's trash heap. Or even better yet, a termite colony's outhouse.

"A real beaut', ain't she?" Hamilton asked.

"Yes, sir. She's a sight."

"How 'bout my roof?"

"You put this up all by yourself?"

"Yep, I told old Sam the Man that this place needed a roof, so he found some old two-by-sixes and posts and grocery belts, and we put it up on the diagonal just like you see here. I like to sleep up top. I like the stars."

"So you're saying you got the top bunk, and I got the bottom."

"Yep, but look under here. You got company."

I ducked down under Hamilton's roof—the top was about chin level, the same height as the cave—and once my eyes adjusted to the shade, several lumps came into focus. They were little cream-yellow balls, and the balls were divided by black ridges. I scrunched up my face to try and bring my mind into focus. What I saw could've been some combination of fungus and lichen, but if you ask me, they looked more like something on a Cantonese buffet.

"Snug as slugs in jug," Hamilton said.

"Yes, sir. I've never seen anything like it."

"Sheee-it, Punxie. They're bats."

"Wow!"

"Moved in right after I put up the roof. Really good squatters. Sleep all day, don't make a peep, and buzz on out just before sundown. Don't hardly know they're here."

"Well, I'm glad to make their acquaintance."

"Keep the skeeters down too. Haven't been drained once since I've been up here. Course, got to sweep out the bat shit, but suit yourself. Underneath's all yours."

"Yes, sir. I appreciate the hospitality."

"Park your car in Moses Coulee?" Hamilton wondered.

"Come on! Where would I get a car? Did a little pitch skipping and got picked up by some old-timer. You've heard of the Old Man of the Woods?"

"Yep, that I have." Hearing the words "pitch skipping" made Hamilton smile.

"Well, I got a ride from the Old Man of the Coulee, and he knew right where to drop me after I told him you were on Whiskey Dick Creek."

"Sheee-it! Didn't I say Whiskey Dick's a sign? Hey, let's check out the still. Follow me, right through the kitchen."

Kitchen?

Hamilton's kitchen was an old single-burner, military kerosene stove on top of a rock and two old railroad kerosene lanterns on top of more rocks. He fired his stove from an old five-gallon kerosene can and filled his stomach from a surplus military food storage chest. I've got to say, no metaphors came to mind. It was that kind of kitchen.

Leaving his kitchen behind, we walked along the ledge until we came to another sort of cave that sheltered something else Hamilton had built: his still.

Another Still Life on Hamilton

Hamilton's still was something to behold. Somewhere along the way Hamilton had collected an aluminum box; then he had polished that box so it was now his solar oven, one that shone with the white heat of a hundred suns. He'd also found an old discarded window, and when he put the glass between his hot box and the sun, the white heat of a hundred suns became that of a thousand suns. But Hamilton's pride and joy, the object of his affection, the one he put right smack in the middle of his solar oven was his mash pot.

In my mind, it was the smartest, dreamiest, maddest example of American ingenuity since the 1950s bullet bra. And while we admired his setup, Hamilton told me how he'd come by his pot.

"You see, Punxie, right before I left Malaga, that madre who called me Señor Tambor stopped by. She had that mash pot you're admirin', and when she opened it up, there were black beans, plantains, and carnitas tamales inside. I told her, 'Hot damn! These tamales are somethin' else! But what I really like is that tamale pot of yours.' And she said back, 'Señor Tambor, you're making me blush.'

"Now, I'm truthful to a fault, so I said, 'Well, that's what I feel when I see your tamale pot. How about you take a hit off this bottle of mine?' And she took a little nip and said back, '*Mierda*, Señor Tambor, I could use some of that to clean my tamale pot.' And I said, 'Well, honey, that you could.'

"Course, one nip led to another, and as we passed the bottle, her nips got a little bigger. And when I gave her my Sazerac smile, she took a real swig and said back to me, 'What you call this, Señor Tambor?' And I said, 'Well, sweetheart, it's called Sazerac, and it's doctor's orders, you know?' And she said back, 'Oh, I see. That's a pretty good doctor you got, Señor Tambor.'

"I could see I was gettin' somewhere, so I gave her my Sazerac smile again, only this time I turned it up full blast. And then she took a gulp and in no time she was really glowin,' if you know what I mean. I said, 'So how about you keep that pint of what you're pullin' on and leave your mash pot here with me?' And she said, 'Okay with me!' and that's how I come by that pot you're admirin'."

Additional Still Life on Hamilton

After Hamilton finished the story of his mash pot, I continued admiring his still. I started by focusing on the refrigerator tubing that stretched from the mash pot's lid to an empty one-gallon paint can, what shiners call the thumper, and another length of tubing that stretched from the one-gallon can to an empty five-gallon paint bucket, what shiners call the condenser. Inside the condenser, more tubing coiled around and around and around until what shiners call the worm came out the bottom of the five-gallon bucket. And right below the worm was a quart pickle jar for catching what Hamilton called his Westcoulatum Good Goddamned 1794 Freedom Whiskey.

"You know, Punxie, it's time for a nightcap, if that's all right with you."

"Yes, sir. It would be an honor and a privilege."

In preparation, Hamilton set a second pickle jar next to the first and slid both jars a bit to the left, and as soon as jar number two began to catch the drippings, he lifted jar number one to the setting sun. The light cutting through Hamilton's Freedom Whiskey cast a triple rainbow across the canyon.

"All right, brother Punxie, take a hit on this."

I took a sip and what I tasted—and I want to be sure to record the God's honest truth—what I tasted didn't speak to any memory near or distant. Maybe it was like my newborn self's first hit on my mother's milk. Or maybe it was like my teenage self's first poke into woman flesh. And maybe, just maybe, it was like my future self, one day closing my eyes for the last time, but not my right now self. No, my right now self doesn't take passing over lightly and surely doesn't want to go there. More like my future self, one who's had enough of this very tired America and has completely accepted that the bargain for living hard and fast and free means the dark just might be right around the next bend or over the next hill. Or maybe the dark might come after spinning out in the middle of a straightaway with my throttle open to whatever the hell it was open to. Maybe it was like that.

DISTILLING FREEDOM WHISKEY

When I asked, "Damn, Hamilton, how did you make this?" he answered back, "Freedom, brother."

But that wasn't good enough, not by a long shot. It didn't account for what I'd just tasted. And it didn't account for all that had happened after Hamilton first said to me, "Name's Hamilton Chance. Take a hit on this."

"No, really, Hamilton, what did you do?"

"I'm tellin' you—and you can put shoes on me if I'm lyin'— the first night I was here, Chief Moses came to me."

"Moses Coulee Moses? Some guy told me a story about him, and I learned some more at the library, but I didn't know you knew about him too."

"Yep, Sam the Man told me all about him. Thinks he's related to Chief Moses and some other guy, too, some dreamer guy named Smoholla. Thinks while I'm drummin' up here I should give dreamin' a try, just like ol' Smoholla did."

"You'd better give me another hit on that pickle jar."

"Sure thing, brother. Here you go. Drink up. Thing was, I went to thumpin' up here on a chunk of rock, and after I closed my eyes and got a good groove goin', here comes Chief Moses. You see, he was doin' his spirit dance, and while he was dancin', he told me how to make Westcoulatum Good Goddamned 1794 Freedom Cider.

"He said to me, 'Kid, put some apples in a potato sack, smash between two sizable flat rocks, and pile heavy rocks on top so that the juice runs out into a five-gallon bucket. Punch a pinky finger-size hole in a five-gallon bucket lid, thread a lube-free condom through the hole, and prick a pin-size hole in the condom. Put it in the back of a cave and let the wild and free yeast ferment. Eat the leftover apple mash. Drink the finished hard cider, or use it as a starter for whiskey.' "

"That's pretty crazy, Hamilton. But I hate to tell you, this isn't cider. No, sir! This isn't even the same species."

"Faith, brother Punxie, faith, because there's more to this story, a lot more. Don't you know the path to freedom is engraved with good inventions?"

"Sorry, go on. I'm all ears."

"Now, let me tell you, Chief Moses wasn't done dancin'. He sped up his spirit dance and started in on some kind of war dance, and his whole vibe was so inspirin' that I picked up a couple of deer bones—I guess some cougar must've left them up here—and I started wailin' on the side of that cliff behind you. I'm tellin' you, I began puttin' out some swing, and ol' Chief Moses, well, he picked up on what I was layin' down. And while ol' Moses was swingin' out his war dance, he told me how to make Westcoulatum Good Goddamned 1794 Freedom Cakes. He said, 'Mix that leftover apple mash with flour and whatever fat's around. Fry or bake the dough any way you can. Eat.'"

"Have you tried out the recipe?"

"Freedom Cakes for breakfast, brother."

"Roger that, but what's in this pickle jar?"

"I got to say, Punxie, you never let me down. There's that inquirin' mind again. Now, you hold on to your ball sack because about the time the sun started comin' on, Chief Moses slowed down his war dance and went into his ghost dance. You'd better believe I changed my groove too. I started in on a son clave I learned down in New Orleans, and ol' Moses, he grooved on what I was puttin' down, dancin' out his ghost dance, steppin' out ghost steps to my ghost notes, and this time he told me how to make Westcoulatum Good Goddamned 1794 Freedom Whiskey. He said to me, 'Kid, you listen and listen good. Put wheat seeds in a potato sack and soak with water. Throw the sack to the back of a cave and let the wheat sprout. Dry the wheat sprouts in the sun. Grind the dried sprouts into grist between one sizable flat stone and another not so flat. Put the grist in the mash pot and pour in the brine left over from smokin' some salmon. Heat and stir the mash until steam starts. Don't let it boil. Add water as needed. Then, stop the heat, put the mash pot in the back of a cave, throw a blanket over it, and wait seven hours. Add the barm from the Westcoulatum Good Goddamned 1794 Freedom Cider to the mash and let sit. Finally, bring on the heat. Collect the drippin's. Toss out the first and the last bit. Drink the rest.' "

My First Morning of Freedom

On my first morning of freedom, I woke up with a Westcoulatum Good Goddamned 1794 Freedom Whiskey hangover. Turns out too much freedom packs a punch. It rattled my cage. It was like I'd wrestled that American Angel, the one from the painting over my mom's circulation desk, and there was no doubt: the angel had won.

When I opened my eyes, I saw my new friends up on Hamilton's ceiling, the ones I'd been introduced to yesterday. They had left for the night just about the time Hamilton and I went to pay homage to his still, and now they were home all snuggled together, dreaming whatever bats dream. Maybe they were dreaming about some cafe in the coulee—a winghop they called it—and when a cute little bat with roller wings wheeled out, they ordered a gnat burger with all the fixings as well as a basket of skeeter rings. To drink, they got one of those new bug juice malts, a really good way to start the evening.

I wanted to say good morning—"Hey, buddies! Good to see you"—but I didn't. I didn't want to disturb them. They looked so comfy up there in bed together like some poor family in a Dickens novel. I wouldn't want them to think I was pushy and gossip about the guy who just moved in, the loud guy, the one who wouldn't shut up no matter how much you ignored him. I didn't want to be that guy at all.

Instead, I started to wonder if freedom also meant freedom from food, and that's when Hamilton's face appeared over his roof like a child's balloon. I guess last night's pickle jar hadn't done him any harm. No doubt freedom agreed with him.

"Breakfast, Punx?"

"You said something last night about freedom cakes."

"Yep. Not a mornin' person, huh?" Hamilton concluded as he hopped from his roof. "Here, suck on the fang of the snake that ripped you." He handed me his Sazerac bottle, not the pickle jar from last night but his special brew, the concoction he'd shared with me the first time he called down to me about worshipping the golden calf.

"Thanks," I said and after a swig handed the bottle back.

"Hey, ain't you the guy with the diner connections, or'd you finish off the last cherry on that cheesecake?"

"Yes, sir. You got me pegged."

Hamilton smiled and then went over to his old military metal food storage chest and rummaged around until he brought forth a plastic grocery bag. Inside appeared to be muffins.

"Dig in, Punxie."

The muffins weren't as good as I hoped, but given the ingredients and conditions, they were better than I feared. "Freedom cakes?"

"One and the same, brother. Cake's the name and freedom's the game."

Colds from Newcastle

We spent the first few days of our Moses Coulee existence tending the still, and as it was cooked by the same cosmic smile that baked our freedom cakes and tanned our hides, it hardly needed any tending at all.

As a result, we had some time on our hands, so we spent that time sampling the hearts that dripped from Hamilton's worm. And while we kicked back and sipped this purest middle portion of the boil, we swapped stories. Hamilton did most of the swapping.

"Got to tell you, Punxie, this freedom thing, well, sometimes I think it's too big to handle."

"What do you mean?"

"Thing is . . . Ah, you know. Sheee-it! It's not easy gettin' free."

"Go on."

"It all started back in Winlaton."

"Winlaton? I don't follow."

"You see, my granpappy used to tell me stories when nobody was around, and one of those stories was all about Winlaton, the place where the Chances first said, 'Fuck this shit,' and freedom was born."

"Yes, sir. I think I get it. I've been to fuck this shit and back. Tell me more."

"It's all about the cold pits."

"Sorry, but you've lost me again."

"The cold pits and the Woods Law."

"How about just starting with Winlaton. Where is that exactly?"

"Why, Winlaton's a place in England. It's up north where a long time ago a man could get lost and stretch out. At least, that's how it was until the king got all up in the Woods Law, and suddenly a man couldn't just go out and shoot any kind of deer. Or pig. Oh, you could get a squirrel, but you couldn't use a bow, and your dog couldn't help."

"It sounds rough."

"Yep, it was. And you couldn't cut down any kind of tree. Had these guys called woodsers who walked around and ratted folks out. These woodsers, well, they worked for the warden, and we know all about wardens, don't we?"

"Yes, sir. Indeed we do."

"Thing was, the Chances back then was gettin' squeezed. I mean, just couldn't get by. Got sick of snarin' rabbits and started shootin' deer. And pigs. And whatever else was runnin' around. And then they started cuttin' down trees and sellin' the shitload on the sly."

"You also said something about cold pits."

"Yep, I did. Helps to know that Winlaton's next to a big place called Newcastle, and of course you've heard the sayin', 'Gettin' colds from Newscastle'?"

"Roger that."

"And you remember back in the library when I said my granpappy told me all manner of things about the Nevilles?"

"Like it was yesterday."

"You see, the first Neville was a John, and then there was a whole slug of Ralphs, maybe more than a six-pack. And after the Ralphs there was Chuck, and these Nevilles, well, they owned all the cold pits, and they started doin' the Woods Law thing, only this time it was the Colds Law."

"The Nevilles were squeezing people every which way."

"You got that right. My granpappy said the Nevilles had all the land where folks dug their cold, and cold was a big deal, of course, because back in the day, folks didn't have any electricity or refrigerators, so they needed the cold to keep all the deer they hunted from spoilin', and the pigs too. They weren't lookin' to work in the Nevilles' cold pits, the same Nevilles who owned all the land my Chances were shootin' deer and pigs on, and the same Nevilles who were always sickin' the woodsers on them. So naturally my Chances started grabbin' the cold too. Made sense. All that cold kept all that deer fresh, and don't forget about the pigs, so that my Chances had time to sell it with some cold beer to boot. Everybody knows the sayin', 'Disown the queens of corruption.' Well, my Chances were all about that."

"And I take it these Nevilles were a long line of baby daddies to General John, that guy we learned about back in the Wenatchee Library."

"Yep, that same General John who fought a war against the excise man and then turned right around and became Excise John just so he could stick his hand in my own Bobbi Lee Chance's pocket!"

"Wow, there was no escape."

"You got that right, brother. My Chances rowed all the way to America to get the hell away from the Nevilles' freedom-crushin' ways only to find another Neville got here first."

"Makes a man wish he was never born."

"Or makes a man pray."

"I don't follow. Pray about what?"

"You see, Punxie, I once asked my granpappy why we didn't go to church, and you know what he said?"

"No, sir, I truly don't."

"He said, 'Hammie, you don't need no church. Us Chances never been churchy people, and I don't expect we ever will. But if you need someone to pray to, pray to Saint Brigid.' "

"Why Saint Brigid? I don't think I've ever heard of her."

"You see, brother Punxie, Brigid performed the greatest miracle of them all. She turned her bathwater into beer and then walked up on the lager."

DREAMING OF BOBBI LEE

When I went to bed that night, my head was spinning with Hamilton's Freedom Whiskey, the Moses Coulee air, and everything we'd talked about. All Hamilton had said about the Woods Law, the cold pits, the Nevilles, the Chances, and even Saint Brigid had conjured the spirit of Hamilton's three-times great-grandfather, Bobbi Lee Chance. When I woke up, I grabbed the spiral notebook in my backpack and wrote down my dream.

Two eagles sat on horseback. One, an excise collector, rested confidently. The other, a federal marshal, read from a piece of paper. A third, this one a turkey, did not have a horse and instead stood firmly on the ground, listening.

"You are ordered to stop what you are doing, say nothing, and see a judge in Philadelphia on August 12."

"Ye're out of yer feckin' mind. I hae—"

"Say nothing and go."

"I'm nae deaf. I dinna hae two hundred an' fifty dollars for doin' wha I want tae wi' what's mine."

"The summons has been read."

"I got a min' tae go tae Kentucky. Your words dinna mean shit 'roon here."

A flock of turkeys came over the rise. Some carried guns. Others brandished pitchforks. One of the turkeys had an axe.

His name was Bobbi Lee Chance.

Opening Les Guérrillères

After writing down my dream, the one where Bobbi Lee Chance was an axe-wielding turkey, I spent the morning and afternoon with Hamilton's drippings. Later that evening, I went under Hamilton's roof, and there it was again: the loneliness that has afflicted me since childhood. A loneliness I've wished away with a good book. A loneliness I've soothed with a woman's musky scent. A loneliness I felt in Iraq when standing near body bags. A loneliness so real I felt it zip me inside one of those bags, and I couldn't tear my way out.

Not wishing to curl up with loneliness, I distracted myself by looking up at the happy family of bats. They were sleeping away, and soon they would wake up and fly off together into the endless Moses Coulee night.

I then remembered my mom. She was smiling behind her library circulation desk. Next, I saw my dad. He was at the tavern, laughing with the crazies, and before I knew it, I was sitting at the counter in the High Voltage Diner, and Cherry was pouring coffee into a chipped-like-her-front-tooth cup. Right after, she brought out a slice of her cherry pie, warm, so that the goo glistened on both sides, a slice graced with a scoop of vanilla ice cream, its sweet white melting against the tart red with just a hint of salt.

When I came to the end of remembering, I didn't want to leave the bittersweet feeling, so I reached into my backpack and found *Les Guérillères,* one of the books the old French woman had chosen for Cherry and me at the Catacombs bookstore. I held the book in my hand and wondered why she'd said *Les Guérillères* was especially for me.

While flipping through the book, I discovered that it wasn't like *The Juggler,* nor, for that matter, like any other book I'd encountered. For instance, it didn't have paragraphs. Instead, it had blocks of print: some blocks a half-page long, some shorter. It also didn't have main characters or a plot. Instead, it had space between the blocks of print, maybe seven or eight lines worth. And it didn't have chapters. Instead, it had, every few pages or so, a page with a circle or a page with a list of women's names. Some of the names were French, some were generally European, some were Asian, some were African, and some . . . well, I didn't know what they were. Finally, I stopped paging and read the first block of print to my neighbors overhead. It described a woman who wasn't using her labia for sex; she was using it to urinate while other women stood in a circle and watched.

Circles and Names

Soon it was too dark to read, but I didn't feel like stopping, so I lit one of Hamilton's old railroad kerosene lanterns and moved it next to where I slept. It gave off a flickering, gentle light and felt like the candles Cherry sometimes lit in her apartment when the sun left for the night.

I then looked up again and wondered about my bat friends. How was it they defied gravity when they slept? Somehow the ceiling was really their floor, and they had no fear of falling.

I also noticed that sometimes when one bat would stir, the ones next to it would shift, but the movement was never violent, just a natural wave action, one wave coming in and then going back out.

Eventually, I came back to *Les Guérillères*, but as I settled in, I realized that my expectations had changed. I knew that I wouldn't be able to recreate the experience of reading with Cherry. And then there it was again, that feeling of loneliness. What was left was the owl-like woman's claim that this strange book, a book I couldn't make sense of, was just for me.

Intent on solving the mystery of *Les Guérillères*, and maybe in turn the mystery of me—I'd read both *The Wasteland* and *Naked Lunch* with the same foolish intent—I decided to read differently. I had nothing to lose.

I began by going to my backpack and finding my pencil and spiral notebook; then I proceeded to list the pages that were blank except for a single circle. No words appeared on these pages, and the circle was not quite centered. The bottom margin had more space than the top, and the outside margin had more space than the inside. Using my thumb as a measuring device, I compared the diameters of all the circles, and sure enough, they were all the same. In my notebook, I listed the three pages that had no words, only circles.

Page 7 of *Les Guérillères* had 1 circle
Page 51 of *Les Guérillères* had 1 circle
Page 96 of *Les Guérillères* had 1 circle

Next, I made a list of the pages that had nothing but names. The names were printed in a six-line block, and these blocks were more or less centered on the page. The names were capitalized and in a larger font than all the other words in the book.

Page 13 of *Les Guérillères* had 11 names starting with OSEA
Page 17 of *Les Guérillères* had 20 names
Page 21 of *Les Guérillères* had 14 names
Page 25 of *Les Guérillères* had 17 names
Page 29 of *Les Guérillères* had 19 names
Page 33 of *Les Guérillères* had 16 names
Page 37 of *Les Guérillères* had 19 names
Page 43 of *Les Guérillères* had 18 names
Page 47 of *Les Guérillères* had 17 names
Page 55 of *Les Guérillères* had 18 names
Page 59 of *Les Guérillères* had 17 names
Page 63 of *Les Guérillères* had 19 names
Page 67 of *Les Guérillères* had 21 names
Page 71 of *Les Guérillères* had 18 names
Page 75 of *Les Guérillères* had 17 names

Page 79 of *Les Guérillères* had 18 names

Page 83 of *Les Guérillères* had 18 names

Page 87 of *Les Guérillères* had 18 names

Page 91 of *Les Guérillères* had 18 names

Page 101 of *Les Guérillères* had 18 names

Page 105 of *Les Guérillères* had 18 names

Page 109 of *Les Guérillères* had 18 names

Page 113 of *Les Guérillères* had 16 names

Page 117 of *Les Guérillères* had 18 names

Page 121 of *Les Guérillères* had 18 names

Page 125 of *Les Guérillères* had 18 names

Page 129 of *Les Guérillères* had 17 names

Page 133 of *Les Guérillères* had 17 names

Page 139 of *Les Guérillères* had 18 names

Page 143 of *Les Guérillères* had 5 names ending with AGNETHE

When I finished listing and counting, I worked out some totals. I summed a total of thirty pages that had names, and I summed a total of 514 names. I wondered what these pages of names meant, and what was the message the author wanted to convey. I wondered if these pages were a sign, similar to what prompted Hamilton not so very long ago to say, "Leave no roadside attraction unexplored."

FEELING SPACE

While those names continued to marinate in my mind, I became aware of a curious effect. It wasn't so much the words that were sticking with me; it was the circles. When I closed my eyes, the circles were there, distinct but floating, like sky writing. But when I opened my eyes, the circles lingered, haunting.

I watched as, one by one, the bats dropped through the circles into flight—a few fluttering bats superimposed on circles and a few circles mingling with fluttering bats—and when the last of my friends disappeared into the Moses Coulee night, I was aware that the circles were gone too. All that remained was a sense of space, and I felt what the bats might be feeling out in the Moses Coulee night. Not really, of course, because how could anyone really know what bats feel? But maybe for them it was all about space, not the roof or the cliffs or even the bugs. Maybe they were feeling the same way I felt in Iraq right after the bomb went off and before I came to.

Once Asleep, Then Awake

It took a long time for *Les Guérillères* to make me sleepy. I had never read anything like it, but after its strangeness filled me, I turned down the kerosene lantern, eventually fell asleep, and heard a voice in my dreams.

"*O-o-o-o-o-oh!* They're out there."

I thought I was asleep.

"*O-o-o-o-o-oh!* They're really, really out there."

No, I wasn't asleep, but I wished I was because if this were a dream, I'd still be asleep.

"*O-o-o-o-o-oh!* Sheee-it! Stop your starin'."

"Hey, Hamilton! What the hell?"

"I'm tellin' you, Punxie, they're sittin' up top and starin' down and talkin' trash and lightin' up my soul. *O-o-o-o-o-oh, o-o-o-o-o-oh, o-o-o-o-o-oh,* I don't like this one bit."

"It sounds like you're in a bad way."

"*O-o-o-o-o-oh!* They're out there, Punxie."

Clearly wishing wasn't the same as being asleep, so I checked for my bat buddies—they were still out for the night—pushed my sorry bones upright, and pulled myself on top of Hamilton's roof.

"They? Where?"

"Up there."

I followed Hamilton's arm and then his finger until I came to pairs of lights all in a row. Stars? Doubtful. The lights were where I imagined the horizon might be, but who could say? A fog-veiled, thin crescent moon was up, but the usual stars weren't out.

"Yes, sir. I see something," I said. "There's a couple of lights, and there's a couple, and there's a couple more, and there's one. That one looks like it's all by itself."

"*O-o-o-o-o-oh.*"

"Begging your pardon, sir, but I don't think reconnaissance is in order. May I suggest we don't stumble around and fall to our deaths."

"*O-o-o-o-o-oh.*"

"May I also suggest you go below with me. I don't know what time it is, but pretty soon the sun will be up, the bats will be coming home, and we can send out a scouting party."

"*O-o-o-o-o-oh.*"

No Place at All

After the sun peaked over the ridge and said good morning, we got up to see what last night's fuss was all about. *Nothing.* Sure, there was the sunbaked horizon blurred by the sun-blasted atmosphere, but what had spooked Hamilton the night before had left *nothing* behind.

And that's when Hamilton said to me, "Empty your backpack."

"What? My backpack?"

"Yep, your backpack. Me and you are goin' on a freedom march. Thing is, there's food out there, and it's been held down too long. It's all about the Foods Law, Punxie. Look it up, brother. The Nevilles got the land and the stores, and the foodsers are out there workin' for the warden. Like I said, got to disown the queens of corruption."

"Yes, sir. But may I ask what that's got to do with my backpack?"

"Need a hay wagon, somewhere all that food can hide. You in, brother Punxie?"

"Roger that. Anything for the cause," I said and started to empty my backpack. Out came my clothes and personals and then *Les Guérillères.* I left in my notebook. Maybe some night Bobbi Lee Chance would return. At least, that was my hope.

We didn't head out the way we came in, down Whiskey Dick Creek and then out to Palisades Road. Instead, we started up the side canyon, and before long we reached the top. Here, the basalt gave way to a weak excuse for soil, and for a while

Hamilton and I walked among hip-high sagebrush, a few topping out just above our heads, and knee-high bitterbrush, some losing the last of their yellow flowers.

As we walked, Hamilton pulled loose a bunch of needle-and-thread grass tops. He stuck one between his thumb and index finger and threw it my way. The seed head stuck in my shirt. He then tossed another, followed by a bunch more. Soon, I looked like some dart board in a tavern, and I smiled at the thing Hamilton had done. He was proud of himself, too, a bit of fun play for a good day.

After that, we came to another canyon, a fairly shallow one, and I asked Hamilton if we were heading along the ridge and, if so, which way. If not, were we heading down into the canyon, and maybe we might even head up the other side?

"You see down there, Punxie?"

"Yes, sir."

"Well, down there's Straight Hollow."

"Okay."

"See 'cross to the other side?"

"I do."

"Thing is, that's no place at all. We're goin' there. If that's all right with you, of course."

"Yes, sir. Lead on."

The other side was more shrub steppe with more sagebrush and bitterbrush and needle-and-thread grass, but we could also see something in the distance that looked cultivated. Eventually we came to a dirt road that ran along one side of a wheat field, one that reminded me of some company-owned timber tract ready to be clear-cut.

Things got more natural again when the dirt road turned away from the wheat field and back into some more friendly sagebrush, forgiving bitterbrush, and live-and-let-live needle-and-thread grass. But soon that dirt road became a single-lane gravel road, and then that gravel road came to a dead-end T with another gravel road, only this new road was double lane and had another wheat field running down one side.

All this time, Hamilton and I didn't say a word. I'd only been introduced to Hamilton's quiet side once, that time we'd left the Wenatchee Public Library, and he'd walked off in search of a free state. Other than that, he always seemed to have something to say, so much so, in fact, that I'd gotten good at punctuating his soliloquies with well-placed "yes, sirs" and "go ons" and an occasional "I don't know what to say."

And it stayed that way, at least until the road turned ninety degrees, cut straight down the middle of another wheat field, and led to the edge of a cliff, the sight of which broke whatever was clogging up Hamilton's works. "See over there, Punxie?"

"Yes, sir."

"If we go straight, looks like the end of the world?"

"Sure, I see that."

"That's where we're goin', brother, right off the edge."

Rock Island Creek

The end of the world didn't turn out to be as bad as it looked. Although the plateau dropped into a considerable canyon, we found a manageable route on the diagonal, and when we reached the bottom, we hopped over what I thought to be a sad excuse for a creek. There were no willows along its banks and certainly no cottonwoods. No animals. Not even a lone snake or lizard. It was only a gravelly memory of a creek, and a repressed drainage at that.

"I got to ask, Hamilton, has anybody gone to the trouble of naming this place? I still can't believe someone bothered with Whiskey Dick Creek."

"Rock Island Creek," Hamilton said and continued on.

As we picked our way over the basalt outwash and sparse scrub, the sun hung over our heads like a blowtorch intent on burning weeds like us from the face of the earth, and we walked. An occasional stunted sagebrush greedily clutched the last moisture like it was the end times—which maybe it was; who's to say—and we walked. The silhouette of a bird came into view, crossed overhead, and disappeared over the opposite canyon wall. Apparently, it had someplace to go, and Rock Island Creek wasn't it. And we walked.

At one point we came to a little-used ATV track and then to a few scrubby trees, ones that looked at us blow-ins with suspicion because our skins were not sun-thickened, and our souls were less ingrown. Not much farther we came to a shanty town of abandoned migrant worker shacks all arranged in a rectangle. One short end of the rectangle was composed of four shacks. A long side was formed by a few tottering outbuildings. The other short end and long side were suggested by the remnants of a fence. A larger shack stood outside the rectangle to guard the entrance. This shack had a hole in the roof above the entry, and the door hung askew from its top hinge, broken, the ghosts long ago blown from this thirsty gulch called Rock Island Creek.

"Time to eat," Hamilton said, breaking the silence.

"What? Where?"

"Eat . . . in there." I followed Hamilton's arm and then his index finger until I came to the larger shack's door. It was suspended from its hinge and dangled like a military vet's arm, one made useless by an enemy rifle-propelled grenade or a friendly fire mortar explosion or, just as likely, a bar fight gone wrong.

"I think the sun's getting to you, Hamilton."

"Faith, Punxie, or we're up Whore's Creek without a popsicle wrapper."

"Popsicle wrapper? I don't follow."

"For a condom, brother."

Miss Pork 'n' Beans

Because I didn't want to be up Whore's Creek without a popsicle wrapper, I pushed aside the broken door, a closure so dry-rotted that it broke free from its only hinge, and once set free, the door feathered its way to the floor. Decades of dust rose into the air and settled onto our shoulders.

"Hey, Punxie, grab me a can of pork 'n' beans."

"What? I don't—"

"Over there in the corner," Hamilton said, pointing.

Again, I followed Hamilton's arm and then his finger until my eyes focused on a stack of cardboard cases. The case on top read, "PORK & BEANS." The next case down read, "HOT

DOGS." The third read, "CORNED BEEF HASH." And the one on the floor read, "MAC & CHEESE."

"Where did all this food come from, Hamilton?"

"Sam the Man."

"I thought you said we were on a mission to liberate food from the Nevilles and the Warden."

"Nah, just scattin' my family history."

"Yes, sir, I get that, but why put all this food here? I can't see the attraction."

"You see, Punxie, that's *exactly* why. It's here because Sam the Man is the big daddy doodlebug around here."

"Doodlebug? Sorry, I don't follow."

"Doodlebug? You don't know about doodlebugs? I got to say, Punxie, I'm continually surprised by your lack of education. Why, a doodlebug is a man who knows where all the water and oil and gold is. He knows where to find all the parts and is the one who can put them together. He knows who's what and what's why."

"So you're telling me that Sam the Man put these boxes of food in this godforsaken place because he's got some larger plan?"

"Yep! This food's like water in one of Sam the Man's wells, and only his doodlebugs know where to find it."

"Excuse my ignorance, sir, but I'm even more confused. First off, I don't get how this rotten old shack just turned into a well. And second, I don't get how one doodlebug just turned into a whole bunch. Pretty soon, you're going to tell me that you're a doodlebug too."

"Doodlebugs. That's funny, Punxie, because my granpappy used to call me doodlebug. Just rememberin' makes me smile. But you see, this all came about when I told Sam the Man about makin' tax-free whiskey. He said I should doctor up my mash with his smokin' brine, that is after he gets it all salmony. You remember, just like Chief Moses said while I was dreamin' and dancin'. And then Sam the Man said to set the mess to boil and let 'er drip, and after it was all dripped out, he'd sell our lightin' tax free as spirit whiskey for religious use only."

"But all this food—"

"Hold your hearses, Punxie. I was gettin' to that. Thing is, Sam the Man told me that the only place to stash food is somewhere like this—nowhere—and the only people he tells are folks on his network like me. You see, Sam the Man and I are two doodlebugs in a rug, and now you're a doodlebug, too, so here we are."

"Okay, that's a lot, but I think I copy."

"Good. Now go grab me a can of pork 'n' beans. Let's get our jaws flappin' on some good old American chow and save all our yappin' for later."

Following orders, I separated a can of pork 'n' beans from its platoon, and, after handing the can to Hamilton, a most extraordinary ritual unfolded.

Hamilton began by reverently pulling out his oak-handled folding knife, humbly kneeling in the dust, and affectionately placing the tin can before him. After opening his knife, he put the point to the inner edge of the can lid and used his free hand to smack down on the knife handle. *Whack, whack, pop!* The point punctured the can lid. He then moved the knife point clockwise about a quarter inch from the first hole and repeated the process until he'd punctured holes all around the can's perimeter. Finally, he inserted his knife point in one of the holes, pried, and exposed the beans. To be honest, when Hamilton pulled back the lid, it brought me back to the first time I slid off a young woman's panties.

With that, Hamilton put the open end of the can to his mouth, poured in a goodly portion, and set the can on the floor. He then nodded for me to join him, and after kneeling beside him, I lifted the can to my mouth. Bam! those beans hit my tongue. Bam! all caramelly and mapley sweet. Bam! All bacony and salty smoke.

"Sheee-it, Punxie! Don't hog the whole can," Hamilton warned.

"No worries. There's more where Miss Pork 'n' Beans came from," I said, gesturing to the cases of food.

"And a good thing too," Hamilton said as he helped himself to Miss Pork 'n' Beans a second time. This time without all the ceremony. This time—*sniff*—the syrup going up his nose.

DREAMING OF BOBBI LEE #2

Maybe it was sleeping on the broken-down shack's dusty floor, or maybe it was getting acquainted with Miss Pork 'n' Beans, but that night the spirit of Hamilton's three-times great-grandfather, Bobbi Lee Chance, came to me again. In the morning, I grabbed my notebook and tried to get it all down.

The first thing Bobbi Lee Chance did was steal an axe-head. The handle was split but the head was sound. He made it his. He could always fashion a new handle later.

He found a shale outcropping and then went looking for deadfall.

He dragged up a log and stuck it parallel to the rock-face.

He dragged up another log, paced off eight of his feet, and then stuck it parallel to the rockface.

He carried up some rocks from the creek below and began a fourth wall.

He walked the creek upstream and found a blue clay deposit. This he used for mortar and chinking.

He continued on this way for a while until he'd put up three walls: two of wood, one of stone about five feet high.

"Feckin' minger," he thought. "Jus' like me."

It wasn't much. It kept the wind out. It kept some heat in. Mostly.

No, it wasn't much.

Bobbi Lee thought, "A mighty fortress is our God. But feckin' shite, it wants a roof."

Roof rafters were easy.

After marrying a rough hickory handle to his axe-head, he cut some maple saplings. He wove them across. Filling the gaps, now that took some doing.

He found a clearing, put a sharpening stone to his axe, and then cut milkweed and vanilla grass.

He stacked and bundled the stalks and tied them with fresh willow shoots.

He wove the bundles among his roof rafters.

"Feckin' shite! Nae a mighty fortress, but it'll do."

Hannah from Heaven

After I finished writing down my dream, the one where Bobbi Lee Chance built his Mingo Creek squatter's shack, I saw Hamilton open one eye. He didn't say anything, but he seemed to be studying the cases of food. That got me to thinking about Sam the Man putting all that food in this dry gulch shack. I know that was Hamilton's story, but I wasn't sure, so when Hamilton opened the other eye, I asked, "Who really put the cases of food in this place?"

"John the Dipper."

"Who?"

"He ate the sugar bugs."

"What?"

"In the Bible, you know, John the Dipper ate of the Hannah. She had all the sugar bugs."

"Okay, but did your friend Sam the Man—a man, by the way, I haven't met—did he really put all these cans in here?"

"That's what I said."

"But I don't understand. Why here?"

"You ain't lettin' this go, are you, Punxie? You just cain't accept Hannah from heaven."

"Oh, I can accept her. Fact is, I'm lapping her up like a dog does his own barf, but I'm just curious."

"You know, curiosity spilled the shat."

"True," I said and paused for a moment. Although Hamilton occasionally admitted to being full of "sheee-it," he had put Westcoulatum, even if only on a small scale, on the map. Not only that, these boxes of food, along with the whiskey that dripped from Hamilton's still, were real. Besides, sometimes in a poker game, a man is in so far that he needs to see what the other guy's got. So in the interest of finding out if Sam the Man was real, I added, "What the hell. I'm all in."

"Okay, then. Cards on the table, brother."

Nobody Knows Where There Is

I was ready to find out more about this mysterious Sam the Man, but unfortunately, I had to wait because right after Hamilton said, "Cards on the table, brother," he stood and walked outside.

I didn't know why Hamilton went outside. I let a few minutes pass and then went outside, too, and there I found Hamilton staring down the canyon at something only he could see.

"Remember, Punxie, when I told you that Sam the Man showed up and said he found Westcoulatum?"

"Yes, sir. I do."

"And remember when I said that Sam the Man took me to Westcoulatum?"

"Roger that."

"Thing is, Punxie, after we got there, me and Sam the Man really got into it. All I'm sayin' is, there's more to the story."

"Go on."

"You see, when we got there, I found out Sam the Man had a bottle of mezcal, and I offered him some of my Sazerac, and he offered me some of his, and we went back and forth. But after we did that, I started wonderin', you know, like a man does sometimes, and I said to Sam the Man, 'Ain't it a bad idea for a guy like me to be sellin' firewater to a guy like you?' And you know what Sam the Man said to me?"

"No, what did he say?"

"He said, 'Oh, you're something else, Beats the Drum. You really are.' And I said back, 'How's that?' And he said, 'You think a drunk one of you is better than a drunk one of me.' And I said back, 'Well, not really.' And he said, 'Yes, yes, you do. But let me tell you something, Beats the Drum, everybody's the same when they're drunk.' And I said back, 'Hate to say it, Sam the Man, I think you got me there.' And he said, 'Yes, Beats the Drum, you know I do. And let me tell you a thing or two about taxes.'"

"Wow, he was really giving it to you, Hamilton."

"Oh, I can take it. I don't shy away from the terror of my ways. But let tell you, Punxie, when he brought up taxes, that's when I said, 'Okay, Sam the Man, give me both barrels.' And he said back, 'Oh, I will.' And I said, 'Fire away, brother!' And he said back, '*Bang!* Beats the Drum. My people been fighting this tax thing ever since you Chances walked in our front door like you owned the place.' And I said, 'Now, hold on a minute!' And he said back, 'No, you hold on a minute, Beats the Drum. You know as well as I do that you Chances walked in our front door and said this party is our party now. This room is our room now. This house is our house now. This yard is our yard now. This village is our village now. You Chances told us to go have our party somewhere else, and not just anywhere else. No, we had to have our party and our room and our house and our yard and our village way over there where nobody knows where *there* is.'"

"Damn, Hamilton, you got into the shit."

"That I did, Punxie, and I knew it, too, because I told Sam the Man that he was speakin' the shameful truth. And he said to me, 'You know it is, and now *bang!* again, Beats the Drum. You know as well as I do that if my people don't die out in nobody knows where *there* is, then we got to pay you taxes for all the cigarettes and gasoline and alcohol we sell you. You know as well as I do that we can't make the cigarettes and the gasoline and the alcohol, but we can buy yours, sell it back to you, you don't really care, and collect your taxes. My people don't get any of those taxes for where we live, you know, nobody knows where *there* is. All the taxes are for your place, you know, that place where we used to live but aren't allowed to anymore.' And I said, 'Sheee-it!' And he said, '*Bang, bang!* I got you, Beats the Drum.' And you know, Punxie, I think he did. He really did. He had me between a rock and a dark place."

DREAMING OF BOBBI LEE #3

After everything Hamilton told me about Sam the Man raking him over the coals of American history, I was willing to let my doubts about Sam the Man go. I respected Hamilton for taking it, and I also had to respect Sam the Man, someone whom I'd yet to meet, for laying out the territory so clearly. It's not like this sad history was news to me—certainly Washington State had its many reservations—but when I was growing up, historical reality didn't have much of an impact on me, at least not until I left the woods, became an American soldier, and got dropped into the middle of the Kurds, Arabs, and Turks, all subdivided into Suni and Shiite, and further subdivided by region and tribe. What can I say? It's the first time I felt my tribe wasn't welcome.

With this new perspective in tow, I followed Hamilton back inside the shack and spent time with the food stash. This time we got into the mac 'n' cheese and the corned beef hash, and by the time the sun disappeared behind the ridge, I was pretty full up.

When I closed my eyes for the night, it was more than Moses Coulee quiet. It was the kind of quiet that makes you feel the enemy is out there. You know they are moving ammunition in. You know they are setting tripwires. You know they are waiting for you to light a cigarette because that's when the sniper takes you out. That kind of quiet makes it impossible to sleep, and now Rock Island Creek was that kind of quiet too.

While I struggled to sleep, the spirit of Bobbi Lee Chance came to me a third time. Because my sleep was shallow, I woke up in the light of the cold, high desert moon and wrote it all down.

Bobbi Lee looped his axe back and paused. His lips pursed and his eyes narrowed. He was thinking. He was aiming.

Then the axe came directly forward, THWACK. A wood chip flew.

"Feckin' shite! Donna mind workin'." The axe looped back again and paused. "If there's somethin' in't fae me"— the axe came forward—"feckin' shite." Another wood chip flew.

What was in it for him was a bushel of rye that he would put in his still, which would come out as whiskey, and then he would trade that whiskey for pork and maybe a blanket to keep out the cold that was certainly soon to come on like a witch's tit before he could lay fire on some faggots.

There was more than enough timber to cut. Rye couldn't be grown if the timber stayed up. Overseers didn't cut timber. Landlords hadn't seen their timber. Bobbi Lee could cut timber. For a price.

"Feckin' shite. Donna mind workin'." The axe looped back again and paused. "If there's somethin' in't fae me"— the axe came forward—"Feckin' shite." And another wood chip flew.

Good Riddance

After I wrote about Bobbi Lee Chance clearing timber in exchange for some whiskey-destined rye, I went back to sleep. Sooner than I liked, I heard Hamilton call out, "Someone's drummin'!"

"What's that, Hamilton?"

"Someone's drummin', Punxie. Someone's layin' down the pulse. Got to investigate."

Soon, I joined Hamilton outside, but we couldn't see who or what was doing all the thumping. Oh, we knew it was coming up the canyon, but in the early morning light, all we could see was rocks and sagebrush.

"My guess is it's a sage-grouse, Hamilton. And one lonely boy at that."

"Well, good luck to him, brother."

"Yes, sir. But what about us? What's the plan?"

"How about you load up your backpack with some pork 'n' beans and some hot dogs and some hash. And don't forget the mac 'n' cheese. Then we'll roll down to the Columbia, and once we get her in sight, I got another way for us to rustle up some food."

Once my backpack was good and heavy, we said goodbye to Sam the Man's snack shack, and before long the ATV trail turned into a dirt road. Hamilton said we needed to get off this track—"Don't like it, Punxie. Smells like taxes."—and our only alternative was to head back down into Rock Creek's gravelly drainage. When we came to a culvert—"That's the highway up there, Punxie!"—we passed through to a stretch of railroad tracks and, just beyond that, the broad expanse of the Columbia River.

"All bricked up, Punxie."

"How's that, Hamilton?"

"All collared behind that Rock Island Dam."

"It makes me sad, Hamilton. It really does. We build dams and cut down trees and blow up villages, but I don't want any of that. The posters in school and the Army recruiter said I'd feel good, but I never did, not for a single second."

"America, brother Punxie. Love her or shove her." Hamilton's smile was bittersweet and fatherly, some might say lovingly ironic, if there is such a thing.

"Which way, Hamilton? Left, right, or swim?"

"Aimin' to the right."

"Yes, sir."

After saying good riddance to Rock Island Creek, we began to follow the rails upstream. The brightness of the late morning was infused with the toxic fumes wafting up from the railroad ties, and it wasn't long before Hamilton found some fishing line. It was hung up in some willows and had a hook on one end. Farther along we came upon even more line, this time with a fishing spoon.

"Don't much like crossin' the highway, Punxie, but it's the only way to the other side."

"That seems reasonable," I replied. After we crossed the highway, we came upon a fishing access, walked through its empty parking lot, and stopped when we encountered a concrete public toilet that looked to me like a World War II German pillbox defending Omaha Beach. Someone had tagged it with the words "QUEEN GHOSTED" and "NOT FOR SALE" and "BETWEEN TWO KNEES." They had also spray-painted it with several images: a speckled egg with two legs breaking out, a pipe with a broken stem, and a face with a bandanna mask.

"There's some freedom of speech for you, Hamilton."

"That it is, brother." But his eyes were more fixed on the pond beyond.

THE OTHER WAY TO BASS FISH

Once at the water's edge, Hamilton handed me the fishing line with the hook on the end—he kept the spoon for himself—and said, "How about hot dogs, Punxie?"

"Are you hungry?"

"Yep. I eat some. You eat some. Fish eat some."

"You want to use hot dogs for bait?"

"What's good for the moose is good for the panda."

"I suppose it's worth a try."

With that, Hamilton went to puncturing the can, prying back the lid, reaching in, and pulling out a hot dog. He held it like a penis and a pickle at the same time and crammed the whole thing in his mouth. After he swallowed, he handed the can to me. I pulled out another hot dog, crammed it in my mouth, closed my eyes, and chewed. When I opened my eyes, Hamilton took the can back, pulled out another hot dog, and slid it down his throat. The juice ran from the corners of his mouth. I took out another, crammed, and chewed. He was next. Then it was me.

"Okay, Punxie! Time to bait up." Hamilton reached into the can, pulled out the last hot dog, and tore a chunk off. "Here. Hook into this and toss it out as far as you can."

I did as I was told, and after we watched it splash, Hamilton tore off another chunk, baited the spoon on the end of his line, and gave it a toss into the algae-filled waters.

And we waited. And waited some more. We waited the way a guy waits in a diner after he's ordered some juicy ribs, hears the waitress shout, "One first lady!" and waits for his ribs to arrive. We waited the way a guy waits after his girl leaves to put on something more comfortable. We waited the way a guy waits after—*Bang!* Hamilton got a hit and pulled in a large mouth bass: *flop, flop, flop,* and then, *bang!* I got a hit and pulled in another: *slither, slide, slither.*

Once the fish settled down, Hamilton disappeared over a nearby hill—"Be right back, Punxie!"—and when he came back, he had a stick with him. He used the stick to bonk his bass on the head, and after that he bonked mine. Those fish didn't know what hit them, which was a pretty good thing because Hamilton proceeded to give them the Jack the Ripper treatment. When he was finished, he put his rough version of filets in the empty can, the one from where we'd evicted the hot dogs.

"Here Bassy, Bassy!" Hamilton yelled as he launched another hot dog piece through the high Columbia Gorge sky. *Splash!*

No sooner had the ripples subsided than a voice came down from the concrete public toilet. "Any luck, Beats the Drum?"

"Hey, look! It's Sam the Man. What're you doin' here?" Hamilton yelled.

"I got some salmon brine for your next batch, but you weren't up Whiskey Dick Creek," Sam the Man explained and started down. "So I thought I'd take a dump in the can before checking my storehouse."

"Sheee-it! You got some kind of cosmic antenna."

"If you say so, Beats the Drum."

"And hey, Sam the Man, this is brother Punxie, the fellow whiskey rebel I've been tellin' you about. He just thumbed in from Wenatchee."

"Yes, I've heard some things."

Normally, I like to hang back in unfamiliar territory, read the body language and all, but since this situation was one new dog to another, I went to sniffing around. "Pleased to meet you, Sam the Man."

After a pause, Sam the Man said, "Okay." It was the sort of noncommittal response used by good poker players, and it made me wonder. I asked myself who was this Sam the Man, and if I met him in a novel, what sort of character would he be? Would he be a carnivore or an herbivore? Would he kick a guy when he was down?

I also wanted to get off on the right foot—seeing that Sam the Man had turned out to be real and was Hamilton's business partner—so I thought I'd try a compliment. "That spirit whiskey you're making with Hamilton, that's some serious sauce."

"You drank with your friend, Beats the Drum?"

I don't know what I expected, but I didn't get a thank-you. Instead, I got a question, and what came next depended on my ability to read a very good poker player. Was Sam the Man happy with my compliment? And for that matter, was he happy with Hamilton sharing? Maybe he was mad. In my experience, people get pretty pissed when left out of the loop, especially when it involves something they've helped create.

Because it was impossible to read Sam the Man, neither Hamilton nor I knew what to say, and as a result, the lapse in our conversation lengthened and lengthened some more, at least until Sam the Man cocked his head and mercifully smiled. It started with his eyes, then moved to his cheeks and lips, and finally settled on his shoulders, the way an eagle does when it lands on a familiar snag.

"Need a ride back?" Sam the Man asked. He was still smiling.

"Nothin' stoppin' us," Hamilton answered. "Grab your backpack, Punx. We're headin' back to the promised land."

After I gathered up my backpack and Hamilton retrieved our "Jagged Bass Fillets in Hot Dog Sauce," we walked back past the Tomb of the Unknown Shitter and hopped into Sam the Man's Woody Wagon.

While on the highway, we didn't say much, and when we swung into Moses Coulee, we said even less, except for the few times Hamilton shouted, "Freedom, brother!" out the open window.

ᴜᴘ ᴀɴᴅ ᴅᴏᴡɴ ᴀɴᴅ ᴜᴘ ᴀɢᴀɪɴ

When we spotted the farmhouse, the one that was the sign to Whiskey Dick Creek, Hamilton changed up his rebel yell, this time shouting, "All for whiskey, and whiskey for all!" And as we came to the end of the road, we were surprised to see a Volkswagen Thing parked dead in front of us.

"It looks like you got company, Beats the Drum," Sam the Man deadpanned.

"Sheee-it! I don't get it. Why's it that someone's always got to snatch my freedom away?"

"*You* asking me, Beats the Drum?"

"Yep, answer me that."

"Really, you asking *me*?"

"Yep, why not?"

"Because I was born in a jail cell. The BIA's been watching. The county sheriff's been watching. The state police have been watching, and the National Guard . . . Oh, they been locked and loaded all this time. Who do you think pays the res cop? Who pays for his Glock 22? And his billy club? And his cuffs? And his bear spray, vest, and squawk box?"

"BIA?"

"Damn right, Beats the Drum. Bureau of Indian Affairs. All I do is move from this cell to that."

"That's one cold, limp roller dog, Sam the Man. It really is. But hey, you got any idea what we should do?"

"We take a walk and see what's up."

"Not to change the subject," I said, changing the subject, "but whoever parked this car, I got to say, I like their choice of vehicles."

"What you sayin', Punxie?" Hamilton asked.

"Vehicles. I like Volkswagens, and I really like the paint job on this one. I know it's no classic bug—you know, these Things were modeled on World War II German jeeps—but I like the black handprint painted on the doors and the hood."

"Yep, I see that," Hamilton said.

"Hey, Beats the Drum," Sam the Man cut in. He dropped his smile and went to studying me. "Your buddy's on to something. I don't think the cops drive around in a Nazi AIM mobile."

"AIM?" Hamilton asked.

"Yes, AIM, Beats the Drum. American Indian Movement. And that black hand? It's warrior for 'got a kill in battle.' "

"Sheee-it! You don't say."

"I do say, Beats the Drum. But right now we need to do some scouting. We need to climb up and get the vulture eye on them."

"Guess that makes sense," Hamilton agreed, and we started climbing the basalt scrabble above Whiskey Dick Creek. As it turned out, it wasn't getting to the top that was tough; that was fairly straightforward. But once we reached the top, we dropped down again into the sometimes drainage of a side canyon.

At this point, it was clear that Hamilton and Sam the Man were running this scouting party. I was just a stock animal. I knew my place, so I just listened.

"What now, Sam the Man?"

"Up again."

"You sure?"

"You invited to dinner, Beats the Drum?"

"Not sure what you mean."

"You want whoever parked that car to watch you coming to crash their party?"

"Don't think so," Hamilton replied.

"Then we go up again."

"Don't like it, but okay."

After we went up again, we went down again and up and down and up again until Hamilton panted, "Hey, Punxie, recognize this place?"

"Yes, sir. We're almost back to square one."

"Yep, Westcoulatum's just a slop, trip, and a dump."

From the cliff edge, we looked down on Westcoulatum and all its changes, the ones that had been done since we left two mornings ago.

1. A block and tackle. Someone had spiked it to one of the railroad ties.
2. Four bear canisters. Someone wasn't interested in going hungry.

3. A backpack. Someone had DIY tie-dyed it, an artist on a thin dime.
4. Another backpack. Someone had latched onto a desert camo MOLLE assault pack.
5. A mirror surrounded by plastic Day-Glo daisy petals. Someone had pounded a spike into one of the railroad ties and hung the mirror upside down by its stand.

I'm pretty sure Hamilton and Sam the Man thought they were witness to an enemy incursion into Westcoulatum. I knew better, so I let all concerned know where I stood when I sang out, "Cherry! Cherry, baby!"

Picks the Fruit

"You know her, Picks the Fruit?" Sam the Man inquired.

"Say again?" I asked back.

"Picks the Fruit," Sam the Man answered, standing his ground.

"Yes, but—"

"Ha! You got a new name, Punxie!" Hamilton laughed. He was pleased with my new name. "What you think about that, Punxie? Told Sam the Man about your thing for cherry pie. You're one of us now!"

"Count me out," Sam the Man said, slowing us down.

"Sure, sure, Sam the Man," Hamilton said, beaming. "Hey, I'm Beats the Drum, and you're Picks the Fruit. Try it on for size, brother."

"Okay," I said, "if you say so."

Oh, Shit

"Is that you up there, Punxie?" Cherry shouted.

"Sure is. How's my favorite waitress?" I shouted down.

"Server, dumb shit."

"What?"

"Server, shit for brains."

"Oops, Roger that, server. Just hang on a few, and we'll be down."

As we followed the ridge line to where it met up with the side canyon, Sam the Man said, "Like I said, you know her, Picks the Fruit? Was that her car?"

"I've never seen that car in my life. Cherry doesn't have a car, so I don't know where it came from."

"What do you think of that, Beats the Drum?"

"Suppose we're goin' to find out," Hamilton said. He was annoyed with me.

"I suppose we are," Sam the Man said, not giving anything away.

We then continued down the side canyon until it intersected with the basalt ledge known as Westcoulatum. From there, we walked single file. Sam the Man took the lead. Hamilton was second. I trailed behind.

"Welcome, boys," Cherry said, spiking her words with sarcasm.

Hamilton clearly picked up on Cherry's tone. He could have looked at her and said, "Who are you to welcome anyone to *my* Westcoulatum?" but he didn't. Instead, he looked at me and said, "Looks like *your* gal's right at home, Punxie." Right after that, a second woman stepped out from the cave.

"Sheee-it, Punx! Who the hell is she?"

The second woman didn't answer. Maybe the car belonged to her, and maybe she'd brought Cherry to Westcoulatum, but none of that mattered now because here they were, a couple of wild cherries fouling Hamilton's mash. I feared we were headed for some crime against humanity, an atrocity only I could ward off, so I played dumb, a trick I'd watched my dad pull when confronted with a sticky, often alcohol-fueled situation.

"It's good to see you," I said, stepping forward. "How'd you all find us?"

"You gave me directions, butt wipe. Just before you pulled up stakes, you said I could come anytime. You said I *should* come anytime. And I said I just might take you up on it."

"I see you brought a plus-one," I said in a lame-ass, joking way. "I've got to say, Cherry, you're the server that keeps on pouring." I wanted to lower the tension. I knew that jokes sometimes helped things along, another trick I'd learned from my dad. I also knew that no one was laughing, so I tried something else. "No? Okay, how about some introductions. Hamilton and Sam the Man, this is Cherry. We had some good times before I came up here."

"Sheee-it," Hamilton shot back. He wasn't buying what I was selling. Sam the Man wasn't even in the market.

"And Cherry, this is Hamilton. I told you about him, and this is his tax-free, whiskey-selling friend, Sam the Man. Remember, from Hamilton's letters?"

"No need to remind me," Cherry volleyed. Nope, no sale there either.

"And I'm always in the mood to meet one of Cherry's friends," I said, stepping forward to shake the second woman's hand. But before our hands could meet, she turned her back and disappeared into the cave.

ꝯOYALHANNA

Things were looking bad, and I was working my way toward desperate. Hamilton had fallen into an oceanic trench of silence. And Sam the Man? Well, his silence had drifted into deep space. I had to do something, so I blurted out, "Cherry, how about we take a walk?"

Nothing.

Nothing again.

Nothing, Nothing. *Nothing.*

Finally, Hamilton said to Sam the Man, "Best check out the still. These *two* got some shit to figure out. Not our problem."

Something.

Once Hamilton and Sam the Man walked away, Cherry and I started walking along the ledge. Because there was only one way to go, we passed Hamilton, Sam the Man, and the still, and after the ledge met up with the side canyon, we continued up to the top of the ridge. The sun was beginning to get tired of sterilizing Moses Coulee and was letting gravity pull it toward the Cascades. Soon, it would take its evening dip into the Pacific to cool off for the night, and then Moses Coulee would become a different thing altogether.

"I know I said you should visit, but I don't know . . ." I was floundering. I was a coward, and I didn't like the road I was on. Cherry knew the clear, honest truth, and so did I. There was nowhere to turn but to say, "I didn't really think you'd show up. I mean, after I read you Hamilton's letter, you got really mad. Then I said a bunch of stuff, and you got even madder, and I took off. I don't blame you for being mad. But damn, Cherry, I did what I did. I made my choice, and now you're here. You even brought someone else."

"Blame *me*? You're pathetic."

"Okay, maybe blame is the wrong word. But why are *you* here."

"Because I'm pissed. I'm pissed because you acted like you cared. I let you read stuff to me. I sucked you off. I let you cum inside me." She clenched her teeth and let drop another tear— this one not scalding but frozen, an arctic tear, a subzero tear. "I thought maybe . . ."

"Maybe what?" I prodded.

"No, forget it."

"Forget what?" I prodded again, and that did it.

"No, fuck you, Punxie. I'm so pissed I asked my friend to bring me so I could piss on your little freedom party."

"Okay, you've got it in for me, fine. I can take it, but we're not the only ones here. What about the others? I really don't see this ending well for anybody. Do you? But since you're here"—It was time for a hail Mary. No, more like a hail Mary Magdalene—"why don't you tell me about your friend. You might as well. I already stepped on your toes, but I don't need to step on hers too."

"Her name is Loyalhanna."

"Loyalhanna? That's an interesting name."

"She said it's a creek in Pennsylvania. Just like where that groundhog lives. You know, the one everybody makes a big deal over in the spring when he comes out of his hole. I thought you'd approve, since you're Punxie Tawney."

"Sorry, I didn't think that . . . I mean, you're right, everybody knows about Punxsutawney Phil, but I've never heard of Loyalhanna. Anyway, I'm not from Pennsylvania."

"She's not either, just her name."

"Oh! I'm slow, I guess. But I get it now. What's her last name?"

"She doesn't have one."

"But I thought everybody—"

"Stop! You're pissing me off again. You need to shut up. Remember when I told you to listen and learn?"

"That's not something I'm likely to forget."

"Well, we're right back there again, and you need to know that Loyalhanna's got no use for men."

"No use *at all*?"

"It's because she was sexually abused by her family."

"Uh, that's awful. I'm sorry." I truly was. I've spent my life among rough people. But even with them, they drew the line with kids.

One time in Packwood—I must've been about eleven or twelve—a girl my age was found dead out in the woods. People said she didn't have on any clothes, and terrible things had been done to her. A few days later I heard that some guy my dad drank with in the tavern had disappeared. When I asked my dad where the guy went, he said, "He had it comin'." And when I asked, "Had what comin'?" he said, "Nothin' more to say, Punxie." Then he looked at me real hard. I knew that look. Maybe I didn't know exactly what *it* was, but I could put two and two together and come up with "nothin' more to say."

Remembering that made me sad, and out of that sadness I asked Cherry, "You know, I still don't know what *you've* been through."

"No, *you* don't, and I'm not telling *you* now. But I will tell you this: Loyalhanna's not like me. For her, men simply don't exist. She grew up near Moses Mountain—it's on the Colville Reservation—and she had a lot of wild in her. It's no secret that her daddy and her uncles and cousins tried to break her with their fists and their cocks. She wasn't born to tolerate much, so she took off real young. To get by she's had to tolerate a lot more fists and cocks."

"How did you two meet?"

"When I was waiting tables in Omak. One day, I asked this customer what she wanted, and she told me, 'Nothing,' and just like with you, I brought her 'The Works.' She told me she couldn't eat it, and I said that she most certainly could. Of course, the problem was she couldn't pay, so naturally I said, 'I didn't ask whether you can pay.' And then I told her, 'You damn well better eat all of this, or I'm going to be really mad.' Right after that, we got close, but then I met you, but you didn't stay around, so we're close again. *Real close.*"

"Okay, but why didn't you tell me about her in Wenatchee?"

"I didn't want to, and that's all there is to it. Besides, me and Loyalhanna aren't any of your business."

"I suppose that's true, but . . ." I paused to wait for my next thought to finish forming. "Well, I'm glad you're friends, I guess."

"Thanks . . . *I guess*. Oh, and one more thing, don't expect her to talk to you. And tell your friends that she won't talk to them either."

"But it's not right just to ignore her."

"Oh, it's all right. She'd prefer it. If you need to tell us something, just tell me. She's not deaf. And if she's not around, I'll let her know after."

"So you're planning on staying?"

"Hey, you're the one who invited me. Like *you* said, remember? And Loyalhanna, well, she's my plus-one. Don't worry. We're not going to get in the way of you and your boyfriend. From the look of things, you'll eat better while we're here."

The Nouveau Geisha Hippie

Before Cherry and I returned to Westcoulatum, maybe I could have, should have, told her to leave. I had no reason to think that Hamilton was going to be happy with these two women upsetting the way freedom was done, the delicate balance that he had so carefully set.

But I was proving to be ignorant and hard and pathetic all at the same time, and no doubt I would continue to be disappointing in other ways. So it's no surprise that instead of taking some responsibility, I let events run their course. Why? I was greedy. I wanted two friends, no matter how incompatible they were, no matter how ambivalent the one and hostile the other.

Unreasonable? No doubt. Downright stupid? What can I say? I like girls.

And I've got to admit, after we returned to Westcoulatum, Cherry proved to be as good as her word. She went straight to work. First, she opened one of the bear canisters, grabbed a bag of lentils, poured them into a dented aluminum pot, and mixed in some water. Next, she opened another canister, pulled out some jerky, cut up the length with her jack knife, and splashed in the pieces. Finally, she set the pot on Hamilton's old single-burner military kerosene stove, and soon, Cherry's Simply Magic Lentil and Jerky Dinner was on the boil.

While watching her work, I wrote a fictional scene in my head. I was inspired by the way Cherry's long, sun-bleached auburn hair was softened by the waning sunset. Her preparations were both elegant and resourceful, and I fashioned her as a nouveau geisha hippie whose mindfulness was only arrived at through great devotion. Of course, I was the protagonist in this scene. As such, I was pleased that this nature child, this nymph, was aware of my gaze and that she, the ingénue, was fulfilled by the free flow of my imagination. Wishful thinking? Absolutely. Delusional? Given our previous interaction, more than a bit.

When dinner was ready, Cherry found three steel enamel cups and, after scooping from the pot and filling the cups, walked in Hamilton and Sam the Man's direction and placed two of the cups on a rock. Then she walked in Loyalhanna's direction and placed the other cup on a rock.

Returning, she picked up the pot and a spoon, dipped the spoon into the pot, and lifted a portion of the steaming concoction to her eagerly awaiting mouth. After eating her fill, she walked over and gave me the pot. Before handing me the spoon, she wrapped a purr inside a smirk and then suggestively licked the spoon clean. It was an expression I had never seen before, one that combined a come hither with a threat. Then she walked away and disappeared into the cave and out of reach.

No Shoes

Sitting in the Moses Coulee dark, I heard Loyalhanna come out from the cave. I sensed that she stopped somewhere near the cliff's edge and was standing very still. I didn't know why she came out. Maybe she wanted to see the crescent moon and the Milky Way splashed across the night sky. Whatever it was, Cherry had made it clear that her friend wanted nothing to do with me and my kind.

Because I could not see her, the only Loyalhanna I saw was in my mind's eye, an image of a young woman whose denim shirt was rolled up at the sleeves and whose jeans were threadbare. Her hair was long and black and had the blue shimmer thought of as raven black, a characteristic often associated with Native and Asian women. She didn't wear a belt, and her feet were without socks or shoes. She was like Hamilton—neither wore shoes.

After a while, I sensed that Loyalhanna turned and started to retrace her steps. She seemed comfortable, moving in the way the bats moved, aware of her surroundings in the Moses Coulee dark. Soon, I felt her pass by and return to the cave, the place from where I hoped Cherry would issue forth, come into my dreams, and bind me in her auburn hair until sunrise.

In My Dreams

Soon, I was asleep, and before I knew it, I was taking dream-Cherry by the hand and leading her back to my bed, beneath the bats, below the roof, under the moon and the stars.

I felt her warm, moist breath on my ear. I heard her purr softly, like leaves rustling in a cottonwood. I felt her teeth bite my earlobe.

"Listen and learn," dream-Cherry softly growled. She was a shadow, who turned and moved away, one shadow merging with another.

Hamilton's Haiku

After dreaming about Cherry, I woke up. It was still night, but I was restless and decided to take out my notebook and write a haiku.

Back in Packwood, I'd been taught in high school about haiku. These little poems were simple to write but also challenging. As a result, I started hearing haiku in the things people said. Sometimes I would write their words down, recording the poetry that someone spoke and the poetry that I heard.

I remembered something that Hamilton said to Cherry while she was eating her Simply Magic Lentil and Jerky Dinner. He often had a way of saying things. Sometimes those sayings were delightful; other times they were just crazy. I thought these words of his were charming, so I wrote them down in my

notebook and then read back over what I had written and marveled: a haiku.

> *Thanks for the grub. Way*
> *over the state line. See you*
> *two in the morning.*

DREAMING OF BOBBI LEE #4

After I finished Hamilton's haiku, I put my notebook away and
went back to sleep.

I hoped that Cherry, the one in my dreams, would return. I
didn't care how crackpot or absurd my wish was. As it turned
out, it didn't matter, because rather than dream of Cherry, I
dreamt of Bobbi Lee Chance.

> *Bobbi Lee Chance worshipped his copper pot, the one he*
> *intended for his still. It was a relic. It was a charm, a fetish.*
>
> *He thought it was his mother, her nourishing breast, but*
> *no, it was his tarnished pot. And he adored it.*
>
> *No one was going to come between him and his pot, so*
> *when a man came down the road near his shack, Bobbi Lee*
> *thought, "Feckin' heavy shite, excise man. How they are*
> *increased that trouble me." It was something the Covenant-*
> *ers sang. The Dissenters. The Cameronians. The Whigs.*
> *He couldn't say for sure, but they were all mountain men,*
> *and that was good enough for him.*

But this thing walking his way was none of those. To be sure, he was an excise man, and he knew what to do with an excise man.

Everybody knew.

"Feckin' shite. Where d'ye think yer goin'?"

"Out of my way."

"I wilnae." Bobbi Lee Chance slowly rocked his axe back and forth, back and forth. His motion was like clockwork.

"Step aside, I say."

"Ye donna hae the gumption."

"And who are you to challenge a free man?"

"I say yer an excise man. I'll feck any who tries to tae my still."

"And I say I ain't. I'm a schoolteacher come to teach the children of Pittsburgh and bring them to God."

"School teacher, ye say? If I hear ye been 'bout any man's still, I'll introduce ye tae the devil quicker than a flea jumps in yer breeks."

He let the man pass.

But he remembered his face. Oh, he'd remember that fandan of a face.

Waking Up

After waking up, I got out my notebook and wrote down my dream, the one where Bobbi Lee Chance mistook the school-teacher for a whiskey excise man.

When I finished recording, I remembered the surprising appearance of Cherry, the bewildering entrance of Loyalhanna, the standoff at Westcoulatum, and the declaration Cherry made about her friend and her staying a while. It all felt like a flash flood, really, but I had to admit that it wasn't Iraq. Yesterday wasn't like that. My ass was intact, but it was more than enough. I had no idea how today would unfold.

I waited to hear Hamilton stir above me. Soon, I expected his body to move about, and I'd hear him grumble under his breath, something about the son of a glitch sun and how today we'd all juice our grains.

As I waited, something else came to mind. I remembered the way Cherry was so beautiful preparing her Simply Magic Lentil and Jerky Dinner. I wondered why she was so self-assured. Where had the strength of her femininity come from? Was her spine made of steel because her foster moms cooked only on cast-iron skillets? Had her spine been tempered by all the times she told her foster dads to fuck off when they wanted to play house?

I wondered about Sam the Man and Loyalhanna. Would I learn more about them? I wondered where they had spent the night.

I was thoroughly engaged in all these thoughts when the first bat fluttered under the roof. "Welcome home, buddy," I said.

After the first bat settled above me, a second bat fluttered in, followed by a third and a fourth—all good friends who had just knocked off work—and finally the remaining bats fluttered in. I watched as they shifted about and wondered if bats snored. I thought about their little lungs and tiny noses. I thought about the way they used echolocation, the way I couldn't hear the sounds they made as they maneuvered about in the high desert night. Were their snores only detectable by their itty-bitty neighbors, the ones sleeping so peacefully above me?

Once I was satisfied that all the bats were safely home, I whispered, "Hey, buddies, think she'll bite my ear for real?"

FIRST MORNING

Despite my misgivings, our first morning went off without incident.

Hamilton and Sam the Man went to tend a new batch of Westcoulatum Good Goddamned 1794 Freedom Whiskey.

Cherry and Loyalhanna came out of the cave and sat by the bear canisters. They squatted just like the people in old time, sepia-toned photographs of native domestic life.

I watched as Cherry got up and opened one of the bear canisters, but this time she pulled out a bag of trail mix. She poured some of the mix into three cups, the ones that last night had held her Simply Magic Lentil and Jerky Dinner. Loyalhanna took two cups in the direction of the still and set them down, then took the other cup in my direction and set it down.

After Loyalhanna came back to Cherry, I watched the two friends share handfuls of trail mix straight from the bag, and a bit later Cherry spent some time braiding Loyalhanna's hair.

As for me, I picked up a book beside my bed. I hadn't seen who left it, but I supposed it was Cherry. I didn't notice the book last night when I went to bed. It was dark, too dark for me to see anything, but then the sun pried open my eyes, the bats came home, and I spotted the book.

Book Cover

I decided to read some of the book. I could have eaten the breakfast that Cherry had poured and Loyalhanna had served, but I didn't. I knew the jumble of good things wouldn't spoil.

Before reading, I recalled the time that Cherry and I went to the Catacombs bookstore. After we returned to her apartment, Cherry picked up this book and said, "I like the cover."

"I like it too," I answered, although I didn't think the cover was anything special. It's not that I disliked the cover, but being agreeable felt like the way to go, so I followed up by saying, "What do you like about it?"

"I don't know. I just do. Do I have to have a reason?"

"Not necessarily. I was just wondering."

"Well, do *you* have a reason?" Cherry questioned. I had trouble determining if she was teasing me or simply annoyed. I seemed to be having this trouble a lot.

"Uh, well, the title's sexy, *The Pure and the Impure*. And there's a half-naked lady on the cover. I can see her nipple."

"Want to see *my* nipple? I'm better than the girl on the cover."

I didn't answer with words. Instead, I answered with a kiss, and she responded by pulling my tongue deep into her mouth.

It was a sweet memory, our conversation and what came next, but then I remembered what happened soon after. I read Hamilton's letter to her and pissed her off.

Reading

When I started reading, I skipped the introduction and dove straight into chapter 1. I found myself in a big-city loft, but it wasn't the old, abandoned New York industrial kind with rats nosing around and water dripping. No, this place was new and penthousey with lots of glass, and there was a balcony with Chinesey wall hangings and a grand piano and Japanesey futons and a bunch of plants. And then I hit the opium smoke. It was all mushroomy and chocolatey and went all the way to ceiling. I began to wonder what had I gotten myself into? Maybe I should have started with breakfast.

But despite all this, I kept on going. I read about a man who offered Colette—she was both author and speaker—a fired-up opium pipe. Then he offered her some cocaine. Determined to please, he offered her a cocktail. But Colette, well . . . she just wasn't interested. She may or may not have taken him up on his final offer, the one that came from a box of cigarettes, but she did eat him up with her eyes. She thought he was a racehorse.

I read about a drunken girl who repeatedly *said* she was going to give Colette the evil eye.

I read about a character named Charlotte who started singing up on the balcony and then about her gigolo who yelled at her to *stop singing*.

I read about a boy who threw off his coat, put on a shadowy Japanese bathrobe, and suckled opium smoke from the nearest pipe.

I read about a woman draped in fox furs and how she slept with the drunken girl, their sleep cast in bronze.

I read about Charlotte giving Colette a ride home.

After that, I jumped straight into chapter 2. I wondered what exactly getting a ride home entailed. Then I read about Charlotte bumping into Colette when Colette was busy selling books. This chance encounter led to Colette dedicating one of her books to Charlotte, which led to Charlotte telling Colette her routine for visiting the opium den. This information led to Colette showing up at the opium den, which, of course, led to Charlotte explaining something. Here is my loose translation: Charlotte said our feelings are a whore, but our bodies are a pimp.

Bang! I stopped reading. I needed some time to think. I could see it up on the marquee of the Bijou in some Columbia Plateau ghost town, someplace like Supplee or even Alstown.

OUR FEELINGS ARE A WHORE

OUR BODIES ARE A PIMP

As it turned out, thinking about it didn't help because the more I thought, the less it made sense, and as I thought even more, all that happened was my thinking was replaced by wanting Cherry.

STILL LIFE WITH NIPPLE

Of course, I knew that wanting isn't having, but I got frustrated anyway. I didn't want to be frustrated, so I distracted myself by grabbing the cup of trail mix and pouring the oats, nuts, and dried fruit into my mouth. I chewed some serious chews. The chomping and munching temporarily occupied my mind.

After the cup was empty, I found a plastic milk jug, the one Hamilton and I stored our seep water in. We could have just dipped our cups directly into the galvanized stock tank, but we didn't. Instead, we separated our straight-up drinking water from our whiskey-making water. We could have skipped this extra step. Had we done this, nothing would have changed, but Hamilton said keeping our whiskey water separate was good juju, so we planted the idea and watered it and watched over it. We did this because it suited us.

After filling the empty cup, I took a long, cool, satisfying drink, but then Cherry came back to mind. I thought about the way her bangs lay just above her eyes. Her bangs were a bit askew because she'd cut them herself. She'd used a pair of schoolgirl scissors with sparkly handles.

I thought about the time her breath was laced with onions and peanut butter, richly moist and infused with an earthy sweetness, just a bit sulfurous, my head in her lap, her face a tanned Madonna with a blood moon for a halo.

I imagined the form of her breast resting against her chest and arm, a subtle softness, accepting gravity as a friend. The painting might be called *Still Life with Nipple*.

After all this thinking and imagining, I went back to my bed and lay down. I looked up to see the bats lazing away the afternoon.

I heard Hamilton and Sam the Man busily moving the ingredients and apparatus about the still. I hoped that soon we would be drinking and laughing together. I wished for it to be only a matter of time.

I saw Loyalhanna quietly come out from the cave again, stopping at the cliff's edge and casting her gaze up and down this little patch of coulee and into that boundless sweep of sky. Just as quietly, I saw her return to the cave.

I did all of that and then decided to ignore my previous confusion, the one I had with the book, and went back to the story of Charlotte and how her bitter bath was drawn from so many sweet lies.

I read about X and how Don Juan counted instead of felt, always with weapon drawn, gorging himself on anchovies.

Then I read something about men running to women out of their closets, so I stopped reading. Again, I really wasn't sure what to think, but there it was for a second time, the marquee of the Bijou repeating something from *The Pure and the Impure*.

RUN OUT OF THE CLOSET

What the hell? I'd gone from thoughtful to frustrated to nostalgic back to frustrated and finally to straight-up bewildered. I was exhausted. I was done reading *The Pure and Impure*, at least for the day, and then I fell asleep.

DREAMING OF BOBBI LEE #5

My sleep was not a night sleep. It was a day sleep, and a fitful one at that. An angry sun shone around the edges of the railroad tie structure. I lay flat on my back, rigid, and above me was a hard black. When I woke up, it was difficult to get my joints to work, but eventually my hand made its way to my backpack, found my notebook and pencil, and began to write.

Crack. Crack. Crack. Crack. Crack.

Gunpowder smoke lay above the turkeys' heads. They had sent a volley up General Neville's Bower Hill. Yes, their fire had been returned.

The turkeys were angry. The day before, General John Neville had shot Oliver Miller Jr., and now Miller was dead. The dead man had something about him. Maybe he would be remembered. Maybe that was why his soul had been so gloriously liberated by a misshapen ball of lead.

Crack. Crack. Crack.

The shots came from the slave cabins.

Bum, Bum, Bum, Bum, Bum, Bum, Bum.

A mass of turkeys in motley moved below the hill. They moved from west to east. The mass reversed course and moved from east to west. Then to the east. Then to the west.

An eagle came down and perched among the turkeys.

Cackle, Cackle, Cackle, Cackle, Cackle, Cackle.

The turkeys moved. They were very impressed by the eagle, being that he was a Revolutionary War hero and had fought with General Washington. All the turkeys knew the eagle's name: Major James MacFarlane.

One of the turkeys was Bobbi Lee Chance. He didn't have a gun. He didn't have the means to kill a man with such style. But he did have his axe, the one with the stolen head and the homespun hickory handle. There was satisfaction in killing a man with an axe, making a mark on another's body and skull.

Flint and steel and dry grass. The flames moved from the ground to a torch and into a slave cabin and then to a barn. Bobbi Lee Chance stood with his axe and watched. He knew campfires, but these were no campfires. These were of a scale he had not seen before. He knew whatever was happening, it was nothing to cackle about.

"Dinna burn that cabin. It hae the slaves' bacon."

Crack.

The eagle was down. "She was right!" the bird screeched. The eagle's soul fled.

Crack. Crack. Crack. Crack. Crack.

The blaze filled General Neville's house. Fire danced from the window, the door, and about the roof. Then the burn left, the excise man duly cleansed.

Crack. Crack. Crack. Crack. Crack.

The geese on the hill surrendered.

Cackle. Squawk. Cackle. Cackle.

After the shooting and the burning, Bobbi Lee Chance climbed the hill and stood amidst the ruins of General John Neville's house. He looped his axe back and paused. His lips pursed and eyes narrowed. He was thinking. He was aiming.

Then, the axe came directly forward.

Thwack.

A charred post fell into the ashes.

"Feckin' shite. Tek my money." And the axe looped back again and paused. "Now, yer caisteal's down." And again the axe came forward. "Feckin' shite." And another charred post fell.

DINNER

Dinner that night was a quiet affair. We were all uncomfortable. We were like a confederation of cacti, each one polishing its needles and waiting for someone to say, "Fuck this. I'm out of here."

Despite the tension, Cherry and Loyalhanna prepared dinner. They rummaged around in Hamilton's metal food storage chest. They dug into their food canisters. They found the stash of cans, the ones that came from the cases Sam the Man had stored in his abandoned shack.

Their search ended when Cherry lifted a can of pork 'n' beans, and Loyalhanna lifted a can of mac 'n' cheese. Cherry then opened the cans with an old claw opener, and Loyalhanna dumped the contents into Hamilton's aluminum cooking pot and stirred the mixture with a spoon.

After Cherry lit the stove and Loyalhanna set the pot on top, I came out from under the roof and called out, "All ee, all ee, outs in free!"

Not long after, Hamilton and Sam the Man came in, and we all found our places the way people do when faced with a new situation. Hamilton and Sam the Man rooted themselves to our west, their back to the still, and I faced them to our east, my back to Hamilton's structure. Cherry decided to stand to our south with Hamilton and Sam the Man on her left, me on her right, and the cave opening behind. As for Loyalhanna, she didn't settle in right off. She paced a bit, not making eye contact, wary, sniffing the air. Finally, she squatted just a few paces behind and to the left of Cherry.

A breeze came down from the Cascades. A pebble rolled down from the cliff above the cave and onto the roof. Cherry then walked up to Hamilton, handed him the pot, and said, "Here."

"Uh, thanks," Hamilton said and grabbed the spoon, the one Cherry left standing like a pole in need of a flag. He lifted a mess of the mixture, wrapped his mouth around it, then pulled out the spoon and settled in for a good, long chew. When he was finished, he licked the front of the spoon, flipped the spoon over, licked the back, drove the spoon back into the dinner, and handed the pot to Sam the Man.

With pot in hand, Sam the Man looked to the sky. Maybe he was praying and maybe he wasn't, but after a few moments he brought the edge of the pot to his lips and scooped in one, two, three bitefuls. Like Hamilton, he chewed a good long while, and after swallowing, he handed the pot back to Hamilton, who then handed the pot to me.

I really don't know why I didn't take a bite. Hamilton and Sam the Man had taken bites, but I didn't. Instead, I froze. There was something in Hamilton's demeanor that put me on edge. It wasn't just his unnatural posture, his hips and shoulders set on parallel diagonals. It wasn't just his purposeful gaze, his left eye only a fraction wider than his right. And it wasn't just his bloodless expression, his right cheek relaxed a bit less than his left. No, it wasn't any of these things that unnerved me; it was all of them.

While my mind buzzed like a slapped-at fly, I thought about taking the pot under the roof, setting it down by my bed, and making an offering to the bats, the litter of flying fur I'd moved in with. I even thought about setting the pot down and taking a dump in it, a good story to tell down the road. As it turned out, I didn't do any of these outrageous things and instead handed the pot to Cherry and said, "After you," whereupon she turned and handed the pot to her girlfriend.

Straightaway, Loyalhanna pulled the spoon from the grub and went to eating. She took a first bite, then a second, followed by a third and a fourth, which eventually led to her handing the pot back to Cherry, who also took a few bites of her own. Cherry then said, "Here," and handed the pot back to me.

Finally, I took a bite, chewed a bit, and handed the pot back to Hamilton, who thankfully took his eyes off me before starting round two.

The entire scene brought to my mind an old hymn, "Will the Circle Be Unbroken." Except in my version the words came out, "Will the whiskey ferment golden, my oh my, Lord, my oh my?"

Breaking the Ice

Nothing more was said until every macaroni and every bean was gone from the bottom of Hamilton's aluminum pot. We had proven that we could share a meal, and although no one knew where we were going from here, at least it was a start.

What surprised me was who broke the ice. I never thought it would be Sam the Man, but he got Hamilton talking when he said, "Hey, Beats the Drum, you think you're bringing spirit whiskey to Moses Coulee for the first time?"

"Yep, Sam the Man, and proud of it."

"Well let me tell you, you got it all wrong. Moses Coulee came to your Mingo Creek way before your Mingo Creek came here."

"That's not what my granpappy told me."

"Your grandfather, maybe he didn't know everything. What do you think of that?"

"Everythin'? No man knows everythin', but my granpappy, he knew all about the Whiskey Rebellion and Bobbi Lee Chance and the Nevilles. He also knew all there was to know about Mingo Creek."

"What if I said he didn't?"

"I'm not much of a fighter, Sam the Man, but I'd say that's a pretty low blow."

"Not at all, Beats the Drum, just something about Moses Coulee and Mingo Creek that you don't know. That's all."

"Then you better tell it, Sam the Man. I won't rest until I know everythin' there is to know."

At this point, I felt the need to chime in. I didn't have anything to contribute, but sometimes a man wants to feel included—even if it's only to hear the sound of his own voice—so I smiled at Cherry and repeated her advice.

"What you're saying, Sam the Man, is we need to listen and learn, right?"

"You might say that, Picks the Fruit," he said more to Hamilton than to me.

As for Cherry, she didn't return my smile because while Hamilton and Sam the Man were busy hashing out the early history of Mingo Creek, Cherry had squatted down, Loyalhanna had scooted up to her, and now the two women were holding hands.

What Sam the Man Knew

Just like before dinner, Sam the Man looked to the sky. We all waited—Cherry, me, Loyalhanna, and especially Hamilton—to find out what Sam the Man knew about Moses Coulee coming to Mingo Creek. We had no idea what he was talking about. The time frame didn't make any sense. And as it turned out, he wasn't in any hurry to tell us.

Eventually, Sam the Man quit looking to the sky and brought his gaze down to a place in the center of our little gathering. It seemed like he was looking into a campfire, only this fire was imaginary, maybe one from an earlier time, and finally he said, "I know all about the Chances and the Nevilles and all the rest coming to Mingo Creek. You don't think I know, but I do. I know all about them having church under a big oak tree, but their legs got tired. I know all about them making some log benches, but then their bodies got soaked with rain and covered in snow. I know all about them building a log church. They also thought people like me, the ones who lived there before they showed up, hated God. They thought we wanted to kill them. They had some crazy ideas."

"Damn shame, Sam the Man. No excuse. No excuse at all."

"No, you got that right, Beats the Drum, but there's more. I also know that the Chances and the Nevilles and all the rest came to church one Sunday morning, and the preacher started talking about communion. He said the bread and wine weren't normal food at all. He said it was spiritual food."

"You know, Sam the Man, my granpappy wasn't a church goer," Hamilton said.

"Maybe he wasn't, but I'm not talking about him. I'm talking about the day Moses Coulee came to Mingo Creek back when your Chances first showed up."

"Cain't see how that's possible."

"You don't need to. You just need to listen. You think you can do that, Beats the Drum?"

"I'll give it a try."

"Good. As I was saying, right when the preacher started talking about spiritual food, the door opened and five guys from Moses Coulee walked in. They had on loincloths and grass leggings and a bunch of feathers. The guy in front, he had the most. He had an eagle feather and some raven, sage-grouse, and hummingbird feathers.

"All the Chances and Nevilles and all the rest yelled out, 'Mingos, they're back!' But these guys were no such thing. The only thing Mingo about these guys was their skin was darker than the Chances. Besides, everyone in the church knew General John Neville had burned all the Mingo villages. These five guys from Moses Coulee were no more Mingo than the Chances were Lithuanian."

"Lithuanian, now that's funny, Sam the Man." Hamilton laughed.

"It's no joke."

"No, guess not."

"So like I said, these five Moses Coulee guys walked right up front to the altar. The guy in front had a deer hide pouch, and he took out pieces of smoked tyee—that's king salmon if you don't know—and put them on the communion plate. He also had a buffalo stomach bag, and he poured out some spirit whiskey into the communion cup. Then the guy motioned for everyone in the church to come up."

"This is one far-out communion, Sam the Man," Hamilton said.

"Is it? If you say so, Beats the Drum."

"So, what'd everybody do?" Hamilton asked, though we all wanted to know. Sam the Man had us hooked.

"Some of the church people said the Moses Coulee guys were the devil. Other church people said they weren't. They said the men were a sign from God, but they didn't know what it meant. A few said the men from Moses Coulee were the Holy Spirit, so they came up and had communion. Those people ate a piece of fish. One said it was like his father's smoked salmon back in Scotland, but crazy-ass strong. Then the same people sipped from the communion cup. One said it was like his father's whiskey back in Scotland, but fishy and crazy-ass powerful.

"After communion, the guys from Moses Coulee left, and the Chances and the Nevilles and all the rest started talking. Somebody said what was in that communion cup was a whiskey distilled from a monstrous fish, a giant salmon unknown to them, a salmon as big as a man. None of them knew how to distill whiskey from a monstrous salmon, but they all said it was alchemy and would fetch a high price.

"They also agreed that taxing spirit whiskey was a sin against God and nature and should be against the new country's Constitution, a piece of paper they were all talking about."

"Now that's somethin', Sam the Man. Had no idea. That whiskey those Moses Coulee men brought to Mingo Creek . . . Why, that's what we're makin' right now!"

"Yes, Beats the Drum. Yes, it is."

Bunnies

I'm pretty sure Sam the Man didn't intend for his story to bring us together. It felt like his entire purpose was to put us all in our places. But when Hamilton embraced what Sam the Man said, that Moses Coulee men made the first spirit whiskey, the same distillation that dripped from Hamilton's worm and that Hamilton called Good Goddamned 1794 Freedom Whiskey . . . well, maybe we weren't a confederation of cacti after all. Maybe we were more a fellowship of bitterbrush flowering after a late spring rain.

This turn of events allowed me to relax, and after we broke up for the night, I retired to my bed. The bats had already left, and although I still wanted to sleep with Cherry, I wasn't jealous of her friendship with Loyalhanna. I have my faults, but telling someone else what to do isn't one of them.

But that didn't stop me from falling asleep deep down in the memory of Cherry's taste and smell and touch. She and I were engaging in movements of the most intimate sort. Her hands and tongue were encouraging mine and mine hers, but it all came to an end when, in the middle of my dream, I heard, "O-o-o-o-o-oh, they're out there."

"Ah, come on! What now, Hamilton?" I didn't want to come back to the surface.

"Help, brother. They're out there again."

"Just give me a minute."

"I'm tellin' you, Punxie, they're planning something evil."

I needed to calm Hamilton down, so I rolled off my back, mouth open and drooly, and onto to my knees. I then pushed myself upright and stumbled out into the dark. When I looked up, the Moses Coulee heavens shimmered overhead as God or Coyote or the twinkle in nature's eye intended.

"Sheee-it! Not way up there. Down here where they were before!"

When I brought my eyes down, there they were again, the points of light Hamilton thought were eyes. I knew Hamilton expected me to explain why the universe woke up every night and stared into his soul.

"Yes, sir. There they are."

"I'm tellin' you, Punxie, I cain't go on like this. No way, no how."

"What's wrong with him?" It was Cherry.

"Look up there." I pointed.

"You mean those?" Cherry asked.

"O-o-o-o-o-oh," Hamilton answered.

"What are they?" Cherry asked.

"Eyes!" Hamilton yelled.

"Maybe, maybe not," Cherry said.

"Bunnies." It was Loyalhanna.

Needless to say, I was shocked. Cherry had told me that Loyalhanna didn't talk to men, so I accepted her words as law. I had told Hamilton that we weren't to talk to Loyalhanna, and she wasn't going to talk to us. But then it occurred to me that maybe Loyalhanna was only talking to Cherry, and Hamilton and I were just bystanders.

"What sort of bunnies?" Cherry asked.

"Columbia Basin pygmy rabbits," Loyalhanna added.

"Eyes! Demons. Succubuseses." Hamilton had lost his grip.

"No, Hamilton, they're pygmy bunnies. That's all," Loyalhanna said.

Now I was thrown for a loop. Loyalhanna clearly was talking to Hamilton, and it was her soft but firm insistence that quieted him down. It was uncanny.

"No?" Hamilton wondered.

"No," Loyalhanna repeated.

"Sheeeee-it! Bunnies?"

"Bunnies."

"Can we go see them?"

"In the morning, if you're lucky," Loyalhanna said kindly.

"Well, sheee-it. I'm always lucky."

"Then you won't see them," Loyalhanna said, changing course.

"No? Why not?"

"Because it's not up to you. It's up to them. You want to see the bunnies?"

"You know I do."

"Then maybe you'll be lucky. Maybe you won't."

"Well, I'll be damned. Bunnies, you say?" Hamilton said. He was bemused.

"Bunnies," Loyalhanna assured.

Dreaming of Bobbi Lee #6

Once Hamilton was settled, I wondered about what I'd just witnessed. Cherry had made it clear that her friend wanted nothing to do with men, but we all watched and listened as Loyalhanna made an exception. I had to admit that Hamilton was exceptional. It seemed that Loyalhanna felt a certain kinship with Hamilton—it was no secret that neither of them wore shoes—and maybe their shared rejection of footwear made all the difference. Furthermore, maybe this kinship altered the way they approached the battle of the sexes. Maybe not wearing shoes was some sign that Hamilton and Loyalhanna were non-combatants.

But all the tumult over the bunnies had made me very tired, so I looked forward to falling asleep again and dreaming of Cherry in the most intimate of ways.

Unfortunately, that didn't happen. Instead, I dreamed of Bobbi Lee Chance, and when I woke up in the morning, I wrote it all down.

Bobbi Lee Chance stood apart from the action. He was under some trees: a big chestnut, some middling oaks, and some saplings. He was curious. It appeared that a funeral was in progress.

A flock of turkeys formed a semicircle around a bundle and a hole in the ground. The turkeys moved very little. They were serious turkeys.

One turkey stood apart. Butterflies came from this turkey's beak and fluttered together toward the Monongahela River.

Four turkeys came to the bundle, two on one side and two on the other. The bundle was swaddled as if it were a newborn, but it wasn't an infant. It was too wide and much too long.

The four lifted the bundle, and although it was a strain, they delivered it deliberately and with the utmost care down into the hole.

Bobbi Lee was surprised to see five ravens overhead. The ravens circled and landed on the other side of the hole from the very solemn turkeys.

Wearing eagle, sage-grouse, and hummingbird feathers, the raven closest to the hole, and therefore closest to the turkeys, dropped something solid from his wing into the hole. Bobbi Lee wondered what that something was.

He had heard about strange goings on at the Mingo Creek Presbyterian Church, something about a communion service done with smoked salmon and spirit whiskey. Maybe the something solid was a chunk of the smoked salmon he'd heard about. Maybe the ravens were the strange men who performed the communion service.

After dropping what might have been smoked salmon, the same raven, the one with eagle feather, poured something liquid from his wing into the hole. Maybe the liquid was the spirit whiskey he'd heard about.

Then the raven who was closest to the hole and to the now-restless turkeys, the raven who had dropped and poured something into the hole, took three hops and rose into the sky.

Quork. Quork. Quork.

The other ravens rose and followed it up and back over the trees behind Bobbi Lee.

Bobbi Lee Chance knew what he knew. He had heard that the man in the bundle was Major James MacFarlane, a Revolutionary War hero and whiskey rebel, and he knew that he'd watched the man fall.

He also knew that he loved his copper distilling pot, and he'd "feck any who tries to tae my money."

Seeing the Bunnies

After writing my dream down, the one where Bobbi Lee Chance witnessed the burial of Whiskey Rebel Major James MacFarlane, I lay for a while. I marveled at the way our minds make stories from our experiences. Then, in an endless chain, our minds make other stories from those first stories. It happens when we're awake. It happens while we're asleep. It happens even after we're dead, the living spinning yarns from the rag wool that our minds have left behind.

My reverie was broken when I heard Cherry call out, "Trail mix!"

I got up, stretched, and walked out into a military sun, one that was on a forced march up our Moses Coulee sky.

"Morning." I smiled. I liked what I saw: Cherry in her leather-vest fringe, her cutoff-shorts fringe, and her newly shagged-hair fringe.

"Loyalhanna cut my hair. Her jack knife's sharp. You like?"

"What's not to like?" This pleased her, or so I liked to think.

"Goin' to take that cup o' mix with me," Hamilton said, hopping off the roof. "Where's that Loyalhanna girl?"

"Who wants to know?" Cherry teased.

"Hamilton Chance, the whiskey rebel from Moses Coulee."

"And why does this Hamilton Chance, the whiskey rebel from Moses Coulee, want to know?" Cherry teased again.

"Well, I, ah . . . Sheee-it! Cain't a guy wonder?"

"Oh, sure, a guy *can* wonder. What I want to know is why *this* guy is wondering. I'd say, maybe, just maybe, this Hamilton Chance guy, this so-called whiskey rebel from Moses Coulee, is sweet on *my* Loyalhanna. What does *he* have to say about *that*?"

"Well, got nothin' *to* say. Just wanted to know where *your* friend's at. No need to make a federal case because I don't believe in them. *None* at all. None *whatsoever*. Sheee-it! Too early for all this. Goin' to find the bunnies. Follow me or not. Suit yourselves."

I looked at Cherry. I was baffled because she'd seen Loyalhanna engaging with Hamilton last night—something she'd told me clearly wouldn't happen—and now she'd teased Hamilton about being "sweet on *my* Loyalhanna."

She looked back at me, took my meaning, and shrugged. Apparently, she wasn't all that concerned. Maybe it went back to the scene where Cherry demonstrated that, for her, actions spoke louder than words. It seemed she was going to just sit back and watch. I supposed I'd do the same.

After silently acknowledging Loyalhanna's curious behavior, Cherry and I followed Hamilton along the ledge, passed by Sam the Man, who was tending to the still—"Morning." "Morning." "Hey."—and continued up the side canyon. When we came up top, we joined Hamilton, who was waiting with Loyalhanna. I guess she'd left before we got up, or maybe she'd never gone to bed. Maybe she had spent the night up there. Maybe she and those Columbia Basin pygmy bunnies had partied all night long.

"Don't look left," Loyalhanna said to Hamilton.

"Ah, why not?"

"You want to see the bunnies?"

"It's why I'm here," he said.

"Then don't look like a predator. Carnivores make eye contact. Herbivores don't. Don't spook them."

"All right."

With that, Loyalhanna and Hamilton slowly moved up along the flat and stopped. Cherry and I followed and stopped.

"Now what?" Hamilton asked.

"The bunnies are living in some old marmot holes. One's looking out, wondering if you're in the mood," Loyalhanna said.

"Mood for what?" Hamilton asked.

"For breakfast."

"Oh," he said.

"Instead," Loyalhanna said, "look at that big sage bush over there. You'll see the bunny in your periphery."

"Then what?"

"Just stand there. Learn to be prey if you want to be a predator."

Wanting Loyalhanna and the bunnies to be happy, we all became prey. As time went on, a second bunny emerged. It was about the size of my fist. Then another appeared, followed by another. As more time passed, they slowly forgot about us and went about the business of staying alive.

All this made me restless, but it was worth it. As I stood there, I wondered what it was like to a be statue. I mean, you'd be forever standing still while babies in strollers, sprinkler spray, and clouds in the sky all rolled by. I wondered if it got old, all those pigeons on your shoulder endlessly shitting their shits. I had no idea that being a statue was so hard. And as for being a statue, I wasn't perfect, but I tried.

Oddly enough, Hamilton was an amazing statue. I don't know what it was, but seeing Hamilton quiet and stationary for any length of time blew my mind.

A DREAM

Later in the day, I went under Hamilton's roof and got out my notebook and pencil. I wanted to record something beautiful that Cherry had said, some words in answer to my question, "What's going on with Hamilton and Loyalhanna? I thought you said your friend wants nothing to do with men?"

Loyalhanna likes
him, not wants him, but likes him.
Hami likes her too.

When I finished writing Cherry's haiku, I lay back and looked up at the bats. I wondered what it was they were dreaming. Did one of them see a snake, a raccoon, or maybe a bat-hating human? Or even worse, did a centipede tiptoe its one hundred tiny cat feet under the bat's curled wing and begin to gnaw toward its rapidly beating little bat heart?

I fell asleep and had a dream about the Whiskey Rebels of 1794 marching through Moses Coulee. There were drums, of course, and rifles and pitchforks, and one very special rebel, particularly unkempt and particularly fierce, his name just on the tip of my tongue, so close I could almost reach out and touch it. He was brandishing his axe, one with a distinctive homespun hickory handle.

And there were banners: Westsylvania flags, some with six stripes and others with six stripes and six stars; and there was a Westcoulatum flag, this one with a salmon leaping over a turnip pot still on a field of sage green.

And there were the Chief Moses Freedom Riders of 1855 on horseback, coming across the old Crab Creek Trail, down into the Rattlesnake Creek drainage, and then off Three Devils, their horses' hooves throwing up dust and looking so much like a comet incarnate, the tail not just fading into the horizon but also through time.

And there was a meeting, the Whiskey Rebels with the Freedom Riders, coming together on the mouth of Whiskey Dick Creek, its spring trickle outrageously robust, the winter blizzards having cascaded six-sided salmon-colored crystals from the sky.

And there was the constructing of the Freedom Still: the boiling pot, the swan neck, the worm, and the collector vessel.

And there was the pouring into the boiling pot of all the elements: fire from sage wood, water from Whiskey Dick Creek, air from Moses Coulee, grain sprouted from earth on the Columbia Plateau, and spirit from salmon smoked along the Columbia River.

And there was the distilling out of a liquor at once magisterial and coppery and dynamic and percussive and potent and sharp and sibylline and leathery and alluring and silky and sovereign.

And there was the gathering of the Whiskey Rebels and Freedom Riders around the collecting pot, a crystal vessel, its facets fractured within a womb of tectonic pressure, the vessel raised to the sky's very own nuclear crucible, the blood-red issue broken for them.

"Glory be to the ferment," the children, women, and men sang, "and to the mash, and to the whiskey drip!"

A Man like You

After dreaming of the Whiskey Rebels and the Freedom Riders partying right here in Moses Coulee, I heard voices. I couldn't see who was talking, but my mind created a movie, and the conversation was the soundtrack.

"What about those ladies, Beats the Drum?"

"Yep, they're Punxie's."

"Picks the Fruit, you mean?"

"Yep, Sam the Man, still makes me laugh."

"No disrespect, but a man like you . . . Well, these ladies should be yours."

"Ah, you know me, Sam the Man, too busy cookin' up some freedom to trouble myself with ladies. Oh, don't get me wrong, they're all right, especially the barefoot one. The other one makes me nervous. Cain't read her, but she's Punxie's, so I just let her be. But all that don't matter because I got a lot on my plate. Got my still to tend to. Got to keep my thumb on West-coulatum, keep it tax free."

"Yes, you got a lot of salmon on your plank, Beats the Drum, that's for sure."

"Those salmon brine jugs you brought, they're empty now, so I filled them with spirit whiskey. Time to get sellin'."

"We should take those jugs out to my car. First, we lower them down; use that block and tackle, you know," Sam the Man directed.

"Yep, the ladies brought that."

BAH BAH BABAP

That night the Cascades opened wide its arms and welcomed its fiery toddler home for the night. The moon was an eyelid hanging above. It cast down dreams upon the basalt and the sage and the bitterbrush and everything else contained in Moses Coulee.

The bunnies came out of their homes, the holes they had redeemed, the ones dug by marmots. I saw the bunnies munch away on sage leaves and twigs. Of course, I couldn't really see this because it was dark, and I was below their line of sight, but I saw them anyway in my mind's eye. Then I saw two little points of light, then four, followed by a fifth—this bunny must have been in profile—and finally a few more.

Below the Cascades and the moon and the bunnies, our campfire was a pile of sage brush burning beyond our desires, liberated, a salmon jumping from every spark. Too lyrical? Well, as Cherry's been known to say, "Fuck you. I like it."

I saw Hamilton come from the shadows into the light. He was carrying a milk jug, one of the ones that Sam the Man had brought, only this jug was only half full. It was the heads—the still's first high-alcohol offering, the portion of the distillation process that Hamilton told me about when we first met—and because this was so, we were soon to get what moonshiners call a mule kick in the head.

"Top of the batch," Hamilton said. He then clipped off the cap, closed his eyes, and took a long swig. Behind him a bat flitted through the firelight.

We all became quiet, reverential, the sort of silence I associated with church even though I'd never been to church. I wondered why I'd never gone, why I'd never opened that door, and I remembered again that old story I was once told about my greatest grandfather, about him being a Ranter who took off his hat for no man and preached from a tent that all religion was a lie. Maybe it was genetic. Or maybe I was just a goose who looks up at all the other geese flying overhead in a perfect V formation and for some unknown reason says, "No, I don't think so." Who's to say?

Having taken the first swig, Hamilton put the cap in his pocket and wiped his mouth, a slow wipe on his sleeve. "Got something in mind before you all get a hit on this white dog." He handed me the jug and sat down at his thumpers. He pulsed out a slow vamp—*bah bah babap, bah bah babap, bah bah babap, bah bah babap*—and began to sing.

Federal tax man,
tax man take my gravy;
unzippin' my daisy,
daisy it be,
but I'm headin' out,
headin' out to the coulee
to the place where I can breathe.

A crackle from the fire sent a spark out into the night. Cherry, Loyalhanna—she most of all—Sam the Man, and I fell into a trance, so it only seemed right to take a swig. I mean, Hamilton *was* setting the mood, and he *did* say we could have a slug, so that's what I did. I knocked one back, and the rush was like nothing else. This jug wasn't from the pouring of the still's hearts, which I once said was like my newborn self's first hit on my mother's milk. No, this swallow was more like the time a lightning bolt hit that tree I was under, or maybe like the time I went down in that current for the third time, or possibly like the time I went for a spin with some insurgent's roadside bomb. Yes, sir, it was like all that and like none of that at all. It was something entirely familiar and different at the same time.

After that slurp, I handed the jug to Cherry and said, "Fuck me sideways, Cherry, that was something. I just want to go under that roof and peel off your lacy maybes and run my tongue until I can smell you calling me so deep inside that I'm gone from this world. Hallelujah. Hare Krishna. Shanti sheherazingzong."

Bah bah babap, bah bah babap, bah bah babap, bah bah babap.

Federal tax man,
tax man take my gravy;
unzippin' my daisy,
daisy it be,
but I'm headin' out,
headin' out to the coulee
to the place where I can breathe.

"Thanks, Punxie, but I'm still pissed," Cherry said, not looking my way. Then, standing in the firelight, she cracked a serene smile and tipped back a guzzle, handed the jug to Sam the Man, and said, "I just want to do who and what I want. Isn't that right, Punxie?"

I nodded.

"I hate anyone who takes advantage of a child and any man who takes advantage of a woman. Isn't that right, Punxie?"

I nodded again.

"I'm doing this tonight, and tomorrow I'm going with Loyalhanna back to Wenatchee and my job at the High Voltage Cafe. Later, I might make my way back to Moses Coulee. Isn't that right, Punxie?"

I nodded a third time.

"And Loyalhanna might do that with me. And maybe she won't because really, I got nothing to say about it. Loyallhanna does who and what she wants. Isn't that right, Punxie?"

I nodded once more, only this time more slowly.

Bah bah babap, bah bah babap, bah bah babap, bah bah babap.

Federal tax man,
tax man take my gravy;
unzippin' my daisy,
daisy it be,
but I'm headin' out,
headin' out to the coulee
to the place where I can breathe.

Now it was Sam the Man's turn, and he stood there a while. First, he peered off the ledge down to what goes by the name of Whiskey Dick Creek and then gazed up at a sky full of stars that looked to me like diamonds all wrapped in green lingerie. Quiet. Quiet some more. A nighthawk descending, *whoosh*. A snap from the fire.

Quiet.

In his own time, Sam the Man opened his mouth, spouted in a thin stream full up, offered up the jug to Loyalhanna, and said, "Long time to be a stranger in my own land, Beats the Drum. And you, too, Picks the Fruit. You . . . Well, you all are just tumbleweeds. There's goin' to be a big fire. A *big* fire"—he turned back to the burning brush—"that will spread and burn everything you got because you want the wrong things. That's what I see. You been at it a long time, and now I'm entering *your* end times. Not *my* end times. No, I can't see *my* end times. I can only see *my* soon times, the salmon times, but I see *your* end times."

Bah bah babap, bah bah babap, bah bah babap, bah bah babap.

Federal tax man,
tax man take my gravy;
unzippin' my daisy,
daisy it be,
but I'm headin' out,
headin' out to the coulee
to the place where I can breathe.

After Hamilton's singing, we all waited for Loyalhanna to raise the jug and knock back a swallow, but when Loyalhanna hoisted the jug, she didn't chug the rest down. Instead, she held it out over the dying flames and poured the remains of Hamilton's whiskey heads into the glowing coals.

In the Moses Coulee night, a ball of hellfire joined with the vestments of heavenly lights.

But Then What? and Finally

You may remember my first words: "I'm from the dark side of the Cascade Mountains, a place where the American Dream sprouts next to the ghost pipe in the rain-drenched woods." I still like that sentence. I like the way it marries up "dark side" and "American Dream" I think that sentence says a lot, but now you get to be the judge. Be my guest.

I went on to say, "I went in search of the spark that sets aflame the American lamp . . . and got my ass handed to me by an improvised explosive device." Bitter? Not exactly. Just realistic, I suppose. Luckily, after I was shipped home, my head slowly came back together. But then what?

For me, the *then what?* was hearing the word *freedom* blare from every marching band instrument and broadcast from every patriot's mouth. What I heard was loud and hollow. What I felt rubbed me the wrong way and sent me out in search of the American spark.

And if I've learned one thing, America hasn't distilled freedom into a single malt. No, freedom is a complex drip born of strife, fed by conflict throughout its lifetime, and comes in many different sorts of finishes.

For Hamilton Chance, freedom tastes like making and drinking tax-free whiskey. From all that has transpired, I've concluded that it's the tax man who gives Hamilton something to fight and live for. I don't know if he'd admit it—I've never asked—but I suspect that it is the tax man who has animated the spirit of freedom for all the Chances from Hamilton and his grandfather all the way back to his three-times great-grandfather, Bobbi Lee Chance.

For Cherry Kozolowski, freedom smells like making and living her own choices, and her fight is against abusive people, especially men, no matter how unwitting their violence has been. She's schooled me on this reality by dramatizing the battle of the sexes. Although that revelation was no roadside bomb, her lesson to listen and learn blew open my mind.

For Sam the Man, freedom also smells like making and living his own choices, but with one essential difference; his is a peaceful insurgency against *my* ancestors. He is the one who laid out for me America's long racist, imperialistic history. Although that revelation wasn't completely new, he served it up close and personal.

Finally, for Loyalhanna, freedom isn't a conflict against others. Instead, freedom feels like acknowledging and healing the pain and trauma that lives within. For me, she's an example of a life experienced in the present. Although she may never think that I'm worth the time of day, she has wholeheartedly accepted Hamilton for the peace-loving whiskey rebel that he is. Clearly, that's good enough for her, and to the extent that I continue to listen and learn, that's good enough for me.

Will the whiskey ferment golden? In the sky, Lord, in the sky.

ℋISTORICAL ℕOTE

Now that we've come to end of my tale, don't walk away thinking that the American Whiskey Rebellion of 1794 was some drunken fantasy made up one night in a way-out-west tavern by a couple of down-and-outs. No, the American Whiskey Rebellion was, as I said, the time when baby-faced America betrayed its Boston Tea Party roots by taxing whiskey to support a standing army, a military force that was used against the very folks who stuffed its stomach. And if you want to do your own research, I suggest starting with Mr. Hugh H. Brackenridge's eyewitness account, the one published just a year after the very rebellion in question. Yes, it's the book Hamilton and I discovered that fateful afternoon in the Wenatchee Public

Library, the day we panned the internet and washed out a couple of gold nuggets: namely Tom the Tinker and General John Neville.

Brackenridge, Hugh H. *Incidents of the Insurrection in Western Parts of Pennsylvania in the Year 1794.* John McCulloch, 1795.

To be sure, Mr. Brackenridge's account is one man's version, so if you'd like to mine way deeper, dig into a wealth of historical documents, and sift through plenty of cultural context, check out the full report done by Mr. Thomas P. Slaughter.

Slaughter, Thomas P. *The Whiskey Rebellion: Frontier Epilogue to the American Revolution.* Oxford University Press, 1986.

And if that's not enough, do what Hamilton and I did, go down to that river that we call the internet, dip in your dish, swish it around, and see what pans out. Like Hamilton said when we were sitting on that old stamp mill timber back in Blewett, Washington, the sparkle at the bottom of your pan just might put the twinkle back in your eye!

ABOUT THE AUTHOR

Jeffrey Dunn lives in Spokane, Washington, among the towering ponderosa pines and Douglas firs of the Inland Northwest, above the meanderings of the Little Spokane River, and below the basalt cliffs of Five Mile Prairie. Back in his Pittsburgh days, he earned a PhD in English Literature and Cultural Studies, but later moved West to raise a family. After retiring from forty-one years of teaching, he now walks, thinks, and writes, publishing short pieces on Medium and longer works like the ones below.

CULTURAL, PLACE-BASED FICTION

Whiskey Rebel, Izzard Ink, 2025

Wildcat: An Appalachian Romance, Izzard Ink, 2024

Radio Free Olympia, Izzard Ink, 2023

Dream Fishing the Little Spokane, Inchitensee, 1997

POETRY

Hubcap Collection Plate, Inchitensee, 2022